Megan Parnell Mysteries

Missing on Castaway Island

MYSTERIES
MEGAN PARNELL
MP

Missing
on
Castaway Island

Joan Rawlins Biggar

CPH.
SAINT LOUIS

Megan Parnell Mysteries

Missing on Castaway Island
Mystery at Camp Galena

Cover Illustration by Matthew Archambault.

All Scripture quotations, are taken from the HOLY BIBLE, NEW INTERNATIONAL VERSION®. NIV®. Copyright © 1973, 1978, 1984 by International Bible Society. Used by permission of Zondervan Publishing House. All rights reserved.

Copyright © 1997 Concordia Publishing House
3558 S. Jefferson Avenue, St. Louis, MO 63118-3968
Manufactured in the United States of America

Library of Congress Cataloging-in-Publication Data

1 2 3 4 5 6 7 8 9 10   06 05 04 03 02 01 00 99 98 97

Contents

Mystery at Fort Ebey

Megan Parnell scrunched down behind the steering wheel of her mom's Dodge Caravan, which was in the lineup on the Washington State ferry boarding dock. Frowning, she watched her stepfather ease the green pickup and the boat trailer down the ramp and onto the ferry. Her mother, the new Mrs. Darren Lewis, waved at her and Peter through the back window of the truck.

Sixteen-year-old Megan slouched lower, hoping no one would realize she was part of the caravan. Despite her silence, her new stepbrother, Peter Lewis, had been annoyingly cheerful all the way to Mukilteo.

"Look at that," he exclaimed, pointing to a boy on the dock beside the ramp. The boy had just reeled in a flapping perch. He stuck his head out the open passenger-side window and yelled "Good catch!" Other people on the dock stared up at them. She grimaced. Why couldn't Peter just be quiet? On the backseat, Peter's dog, Jiggs, a big, black mix of several breeds, bounced back and forth from one window to the other. Shedding hair all over the van, probably.

Megan never turned down a chance to use her new driver's license, but right now she wished she were anywhere but behind the wheel of this minivan, going anywhere but on this camping trip. That anywhere, preferably, would be with her friends from church at their end-of-summer bash at the lake. That cute new boy, Sean Bertram, had asked if she planned to come—in a way that made her think he wasn't just making conversation.

The ferry attendant signaled her into an inside lane. Megan drove forward, past the pickup and trailer, which had parked against the outside wall of the ferry. She held her breath for fear she might scrape the center wall.

Peter interrupted her concentration. "You're fine on this side," he said cheerfully. "Lots of room."

"Do you mind?" she snapped. "I'm doing the driving." She pulled up behind the car ahead, put the van in park, and yanked the emergency brake.

Peter recoiled in mock horror. "Whoa! I was just trying to help." He grinned, showing his braces. "Are you coming upstairs?"

Megan looked at Peter with the same enthusiasm she reserved for a squashed bug. "No."

His grin disappeared. He shrugged. "Suit yourself."

Megan pushed aside a twinge of guilt. Peter did know a lot about cars and was a good driver, even if he wasn't old enough for his license. But this wasn't about driving. She and her mom had always managed fine on their own. Why couldn't things just stay the same?

In the backseat, Jiggs' tail pounded the upholstery. Peter slid out of the van and reached over the seat to rub the dog's speckled muzzle. "Sorry, boy. Dogs stay on the car deck."

Megan watched him squeeze between the vehicles

and the wall until he reached the forward stairway to the passenger deck. Peter was okay, really. She'd known him forever ... they'd grown up playing together in the same cul-de-sac in Madrona Bay. His dad had often done the man-type chores that needed doing at the Parnell household.

Peter's mom and hers had been best friends, until Jolene Lewis died of cancer two years ago. After that, Peter became something of a clown, teasing and playing pranks. That was a cover-up, of course. Megan knew he missed his mom terribly. It must be hard for him to have someone take his mother's place ... as hard as it had been for her to give up her secret dream that Fred Parnell, her own father, would someday come back to her and Mom.

In the van's mirror, she watched Darren Lewis and her mother get out of the truck and make their way forward. Darren's prematurely silver hair and his slight limp gave him a distinguished look. Both he and her mother were slender and fit. The new Mrs. Lewis glowed. They were holding hands, for heaven's sake. Megan scowled.

At the wedding two weeks ago, people had told Megan how lovely she looked in her rose-colored bridesmaid's dress. Everyone exclaimed over what a beautiful family they made. She'd stretched her face muscles into an artificial smile. And alone in her room in the empty new house that night, she cried, knowing that the handsome father who'd left when she was only four, and who she sometimes saw reporting foreign news stories on TV, could not come back to his family now even if he wanted to. Why did God allow things like divorce, anyway?

When Darren and Sarah came back from their honeymoon, they'd announced that a camping trip would be the perfect way to end the summer and help them all get used to living as a family. Megan grudgingly prepared to go. No camping trip was going to make her feel happy.

Sarah stopped beside the van. "Go on up, Darren," she said to her husband. "I'll be along in a minute."

Short, dark hair waved around the pleasant, pretty face framed in the open window. "I know all this is hard for you, dear. But it can work, if you let it."

Megan refused to look at her mother. She drew in her breath. "If *I* let it? Everything was fine before. It wasn't me who changed things."

"Nothing ever stays the same." Sympathy warmed Sarah's brown eyes. "I want this to be a good change, for all of us."

Megan bit her lip.

"Please. Won't you at least try to understand?" Her mother waited, watching her. Then she sighed, touched Megan's shoulder, and went on toward the stairs.

The ferry vibrated as the engine speeded up. Creosoted bundles of pilings moved past the outside wall. The expression on her mother's face as she'd turned away stabbed into Megan's heart.

A tear escaped from under her lashes. She bowed her head and tried to find words to pray. "Jesus, I'm sorry. This is all so hard. Help me ... help me ..." Megan didn't know exactly what she wanted help with, but she felt a little better. Jesus did promise to always be with her. She'd go topside. If she ran into the others, she'd be pleasant, even if it killed her.

~~~~~~~~~~~~~~~~

Megan spotted her mother and Darren in the line at the coffee shop counter. She waved and made her way toward the exit at the back of the passenger deck. Maybe if she could just be by herself for a while ...

Then she saw Peter, leaning over the railing. His red-brown hair gleamed in the sun. He looked up and saw her.

"Hi," he said.

"Hi." Megan saw the wary look in his eyes and felt ashamed of her grumpiness. She tried to make amends. "It's nice out here, isn't it?"

Peter nodded. She stepped next to him and watched a speedboat cut across the ferry's wake. Though Peter was only a few months younger, she was taller. But he'd grown over the summer, she noted.

"Want to go forward?" he suggested.

Megan shrugged. "All right."

They strolled along the open deck that ran around the passenger lounges. Pleasure boats of every size and description dotted the blue waters of Puget Sound. The breeze whipped her long, dark hair across her face, and she pushed it back. Whidbey Island grew closer by the minute.

Peter spoke. "Even though we used to cruise past Whidbey in our boat, I haven't been ashore there much."

"Mom and I used to take Sunday drives up the island and come back by way of Deception Pass," Megan said. "After we dock, it's still a long way to the campground. Fort Ebey's more than halfway up the island."

Passengers crowded the railing across the front of the deck. Megan and Peter squeezed between a man with a pair of binoculars and a chubby girl in shorts. They looked down on the car deck below. "Dad will be interested in Fort Ebey," Peter said. "He hated Vietnam, but he still likes anything to do with military history."

A sudden, deafening blast from the ferry's horn made Megan's heart jump and race. A woman screamed as a flash of white zipped across the path of the ferry, almost under the prow of the ship.

"Did you see that?" a man exclaimed. "Idiot missed us by no more than a coat of paint!"

The driver of the offending pleasure boat shook his fist at the ferry, then gunned the motor and sped away.

"Did you see the boat's name?" asked Peter.

"Yes," Megan said. "It was the Sister Suzie. That guy's just plain stupid!"

"Not only stupid, he's got a lot of nerve," Peter said. "I hope he's off the water by the time we go out in our boat. I'd hate to tangle with him in anything smaller than this ferry."

~~~~~~~~~~~~~~~~~~~~~~~~~~~~~~~~

"There!" Peter said. "The sign says Fort Ebey."

Megan glanced at the green Ford pickup following them and swung the minivan off the main highway. The twisting, hilly road to the campground tested her new driving skills, but she tried not to let Peter see her nervousness.

Shoulder-high masses of shrubbery separated the campsites. Megan pulled into one of the larger spots and switched off the engine. She and Peter got out and watched while their parents backed the truck and boat trailer into a nearby parking area. Around them, the straight, nearly limbless trunks of fir trees rose above bushes of leathery-leaved salal. The trees' wind-flattened tops all pointed inland. Megan looped her camera strap around her neck. She was glad she'd stuck her sketchbook into her duffle bag. At least she'd have something to keep her busy when she got bored.

"Is this site okay?" she called to the adults.

"It's fine. I'm glad we came today," Sarah Lewis replied. "We got a jump on the Labor Day crowd. By tomorrow, every space will be taken."

Peter let Jiggs out of the van and put him on his leash. They jumped over a big log and ran along a path which led through the woods.

Megan started to reach for her sketchbook, but curiosity made her leave it and follow Peter. The path T-boned with another that skirted the edge of a high bluff.

Jiggs skidded to a stop, his nose over empty space. He drew back. Megan caught up and stood beside Peter. The wide Strait of Juan de Fuca sparkled below their feet. The name was pronounced, she knew, as the Spanish said it, *Wan de Fee-yoo-kuh.*

It stretched westward toward the Pacific Ocean. Megan caught her breath at the beauty of the scene.

"Awesome!" Peter exclaimed.

Across the Strait and a little to the south lay the shining mountains of the Olympic Peninsula. Peter pointed to some purple land masses in the north. "Those must be the San Juan Islands."

"Yes, and the one farthest away is Vancouver Island in Canada."

Megan looked back through the trees to where their parents were setting up camp and remembered that she'd not planned to enjoy herself. "Come on, we'd better quit fooling around and help get this show on the road."

Peter made a face at her. "Okay, boss."

He grinned and his braces flashed silver. "I'll be right with you. I'll walk Jiggs a little more first."

By the time they'd set up the tents and Mom had cooked a quick supper, Megan had almost forgotten her determination to be miserable. Her feet itched to start exploring. "Do you want help with the dishes, Mom?" she offered.

"No, thanks. Darren will help. Go ahead and look around, you two."

Peter untied Jiggs and fastened the leash to the dog's collar. "Come on, pal."

Megan grabbed her camera, climbed over the big log, and stopped at the edge of the bluff. Out in the middle of Puget Sound, a toy ferry crept toward the town of Port Townsend on the far shore. She framed the scene in the viewfinder and clicked the shutter. She turned to Peter. "Which way do you want to go?"

Jiggs was tugging Peter along the path forking to the right. "It looks like we're going this way."

They jogged along behind the dog. The trail dipped away from the bluff and through the woods, then clung to a hillside above a wide, grassy meadow. The meadow ended abruptly in more bluffs. They stopped to look.

"That would make a great battlefield," Peter said. "See, that looks like an old, overgrown trench down there. I wonder if anyone ever fought here?"

"Maybe Indians, a long time ago." Megan pulled a brochure from her pocket. "I picked this up on the ferry. It says the Army built several forts to keep enemy ships from using Admiralty Inlet to reach the cities of Puget Sound."

She stopped and frowned. "I thought all this water is called the Strait of Juan de Fuca."

"Admiralty Inlet is the part that lies between the Olympic Peninsula and Whidbey. It starts about at the point where Port Townsend lies, over there, Peter said, pointing."

"Oh," Megan said. Peter should know. He and his dad had taken their boat out there often enough. "Anyway, Fort Casey is one of the forts. There's another one at Port Townsend. This says the invention of fighter planes made the forts obsolete."

Jiggs tugged Peter along the path. Rabbit trails burrowed into the heavy growth of shrubs on the hillside. The big dog lunged from one interesting scent to the next. "Take it easy," Peter scolded.

Megan followed, still studying her brochure. "It says the fortifications here were sort of a political afterthought. Hmm."

Jiggs' whole body disappeared into an opening in

the brush. The end of his tail quivered as he strained against the leash.

"What did you find, boy?" Peter pushed his way after the dog, who sniffed along the trunk of a fallen tree. Peter hopped onto it and walked behind as Jiggs followed his nose down the log, then along a twisty trail among the bushes. Megan shoved the brochure back into her pocket and hurried to catch up. The trail ended in a small clearing at the edge of the forest.

"This would be a good hideout for kids to play in," Peter said, pointing to another downed tree whose torn-out root system held the trunk far enough off the ground to make a snug shelter underneath.

Megan stooped to peer into the hollow. "Look," she said. "It *is* a hideout."

The tips of evergreen branches were spread on the ground to make a soft bed. Folded neatly on the branches they saw a blanket.

She backed away. "I ... think we'd better get out of here. Someone could be hiding from the law. He might be watching."

"Why would someone hide from the law here?" Peter scoffed. "Besides, Jiggs won't let anyone bother us."

Nevertheless, he followed Megan back to the main trail.

A little farther on, the trail curved around a bend and ended at a grassy circle set into concrete paving. Trees and bushes covered a small hill behind the circle. A concrete-framed opening yawned black and mysterious in the hill.

"An underground bunker!" Peter exclaimed. "Dad will love this."

Megan stepped down into the grassy saucer. "Fort Casey, down the island, had lots of bunkers and lots of guns. Ebey had only two guns. One of them fit right here, see?"

Peter nodded. He looked toward the Strait where a container ship lumbered north on its way to Alaska or maybe to a Canadian port. "An enemy ship would have been a sitting duck for the gunner, wouldn't it? Let's see what's inside the bunker."

They paused at the entrance and looked in. A concrete wall curved away into blackness. Chambers lined the passageway on their right, some with doors closed, others standing open.

The air smelled musty. "Brrr. It's cold in here."

Peter's voice echoed as he poked his head into one of the chambers. "They must have stored their ammunition in these rooms."

"I guess so."

They rounded the curve in the passageway. Now the tunnel was completely dark. Jiggs pressed against his master and whined.

"We'd better go back," Megan said.

"What are you scared of, spooks?" Peter teased. "This has to come out somewhere." His voice sounded less certain. "Won't it?"

They felt their way along the wall. Somewhere close by, Megan heard a faint rustle. The hair stood up on the back of her neck. Jiggs growled. Her imagination conjured up all sorts of scary presences to fill the chambers they were passing.

"I'm bringing a flashlight next time," she muttered.

In a few moments, gray light washed the wall ahead of them. Megan dashed for the entrance. "Wait for me!" Peter shouted.

Megan glanced back and saw Jiggs suddenly lurch in front of Peter and head back into the darkness. The leash jerked around Peter's legs and toppled him onto the concrete. One of the metal doors in the tunnel banged shut. Jiggs exploded into barking that echoed head-splittingly in the confined space.

"Stop it, stupid dog!" Peter shouted. He scrambled to his feet and hauled Jiggs after him out of the tunnel.

Megan's heart hammered despite the bright sunshine. "Did you make that door slam?"

"No." Peter's face was drained of color. He made a show of inspecting his skinned elbow. "It must have been the wind."

"There's hardly enough wind for that," she observed.

Peter glanced back at the opening. "Someone else was in there then."

"Maybe." Megan climbed on top of a picnic table to peer down the other side of the little ridge. "There are openings on the back side of the hill. Somebody could have been trying to scare us. See, there are a couple of cars in the parking lot down there."

"I don't see anybody around."

"Me either."

"I'm getting out of here!" Peter turned from the parking lot and ran down the opposite side of the ridge, down some steps to where branching trails led across the meadow toward the bluffs.

Megan jumped off the picnic table and raced after him and Jiggs. She couldn't resist the opportunity to throw Peter's words back at him. "What are you scared of, spooks?"

"Yaaa-aaah!" Peter turned, waving his arms like a Halloween ghost. They slowed to a walk, laughing.

Peter unsnapped Jiggs' leash. "No one will care if he runs free here."

The dog loped happily away through the long dry grass. Peter and Megan ran after him. They neared the edge of the bluff.

"Be careful," Megan said. "It might give way if we get too close."

They peered down at a curving gravel beach. "Maybe there are agates down there," she said. "I think I'll go beach combing tomorrow."

"Want company?"

She shrugged, realizing that she was having more fun than she'd intended. "Whatever."

In silence, they followed the edge of the bluff north to where the grassland ended and the hillside rose steeply above them. The sun had dropped nearly to the horizon, sending a path of rosy light blazing across the water. Megan took a couple of photographs.

"Your mom said to be back before dark," said Peter. "If we climb up here, maybe we'll find a shortcut back to camp."

"Maybe." Megan reached for the folded paper in her back pocket. "The map on this brochure shows trails going both ways from the fort."

Jiggs picked his way up the steep slope. Megan started after him. "Deer tracks," she said, pointing to some cloven hoofprints in the dirt. "If the deer can climb up here, I guess we can too."

At the top of the slope the overhanging brush grew too thick to penetrate. They scrambled along beneath it until Jiggs discovered a deer trail leading through the tangle and into the trees. There, a walking path paralleled the bluff.

Peter snapped Jiggs' leash to his collar. "It's almost dark under these trees. We'd better hurry."

They came to the picnic area beside the bunker as the big red sun slipped behind the Olympics. The path across the water turned as red and luminous as the sun. "Oh, it's beautiful!" breathed Megan.

They stopped to watch. Just then, so softly that at first it seemed a bird call, notes of a flute came from the top of the bunker. Jiggs cocked his head.

Pure and clean, the notes ran up and down the scale. Then music floated from the hill—light, airy music that tripped and danced. The unseen musician paused, then began to play a sad, longing melody.

Peter looked at Megan, questioning if they should try to find the flute player.

Megan glanced at the empty parking lot and shook her head. "We'd better go back," she whispered. "Mom will be looking for us." Reluctantly, they moved past the bunker and into the woods. The flute continued to sing.

Later that night, they all sat around a campfire, watching sparks fly upward. A big round moon floating overhead sent shafts of pale light through the trees. Memories flooded in of a time long ago when Megan's own father had taken her camping. Perhaps the thought was childish, but why couldn't it be her father sitting there next to her mother instead of Darren Lewis? She hugged her knees and fought back tears.

Her mom began to sing softly, "I see the moon, the moon sees me ..."

Darren joined in, then Peter, "The moon sees the one I long to see."

Just one big happy family, Megan thought bitterly. She clamped her lips together as the others sang. "God bless the moon, and God bless me, and God bless the one I long to see."

In the firelight Sarah's face, watching her daughter, held a pleading expression. Resentment surged inside Megan. But sulking got old fast, and the evening was too pleasant to waste in sulking anyway.

On the second verse, she sang too. "It is my joy in life to find at every turning of the road, the strong arm of a comrade kind to help me onward with my load."

The words of the old song struck Megan with new

meaning. Her mother had been carrying the load for both of them for a long time. Maybe she ought to be glad Mom had someone to help her.

After they'd sung all the camping songs they knew, Darren read verses of Psalm 46 from the Bible. The campfire flickered low.

> God is our refuge and strength,
> > an ever-present help in trouble.
> Therefore we will not fear, though the
> > > earth give way
> > and the mountains fall into the
> > > heart of the sea,
> though its waters roar and foam
> > and the mountains quake with their
> > > surging.
> There is a river whose streams make
> > > glad the city of God,
> > the holy place where the Most High
> > > dwells.
> God is within her, she will not fall;
> > God will help her at break of day.
> Nations are in uproar, kingdoms fall;
> > He lifts His voice, the earth melts.
>
> The LORD Almighty is with us;
> > the God of Jacob is our fortress.

"Well," Darren said, closing the book, "Jiggs is sound asleep in the van. Guess it's about time for the rest of us to turn in."

Megan didn't feel at all sleepy. She thought about the mysterious musician. Was he still out there? She met Peter's eyes and dipped her head in the direction of the bunker. He caught her message and nodded.

"The moonlight is so bright," Megan said. "Is it okay if Peter and I go for a short walk? We're not tired yet."

Sarah glanced at Peter's dad. She smiled and nodded. "Take the flashlight."

Megan grabbed the light from the picnic table. She and Peter started through the woods. After a few minutes, she switched the light off. "Enough moonlight gets through for us to see where we're going," she said. She stood a moment, letting her eyes get used to the shadows.

"Yeah," Peter said. "If we leave the flashlight off, maybe we can creep up on whoever was making that music before he sees us."

They moved along the trail, sometimes stumbling over a root or a rough place, trying not to make noise. Now and then they stopped to listen. They heard the calls of night birds and branches rustling in the breeze. Nothing else.

The silhouette of the bunker loomed on their left. They peered up at it and listened. Suddenly a sound made Megan clutch Peter's arm. It came from the direction of the parking lot. Again she heard it ... the clink of glass on metal. They crept past a tangle of bushes. Near a trash can, something moved.

"A bear!" Peter exclaimed under his breath.

Megan switched on their powerful flashlight. A thin, ragged boy in a baseball cap froze in the beam. Trash lay scattered at his feet; his hands held scraps of discarded food.

He dropped the food, whirled, and dashed for the woods beyond the parking lot.

"Wait!" Peter called. "We won't hurt you!"

Megan played the flashlight beam over the tree trunks but he was gone. "The poor kid," she said. "He looked starved. And filthy. I wonder what he's doing here."

"The camp on the hill!" said Peter.

"What?"

"The camp we found. I'll bet it's his."

"That's it!" Megan agreed. "But he can't be the musician."

"No. What kid could play like that?"

They climbed to the picnic area and stood looking out at a world gone black and silver.

"I've got an idea." Even in the moonlight, Peter's eyes sparkled. "Let's take some food to his camp really early in the morning. Maybe we can find out why he's here."

"Okay." Megan perched on the end of a picnic table. The glimmering moon path stretched to the west across the dark water, out toward the ocean, out toward ... the future?

~~~~~~~~~~~~~~~~~~~~~~~~~

In the night, the woods seemed alive with sounds Megan had never noticed in the daytime. The moon shone through the flap of her pup tent and kept her awake. Then, as she began to get sleepy, she felt a hard lump under her shoulder and realized the air had leaked from her air mattress. But finally, she dropped off to sleep. She woke with a jerk and raised her head. To her surprise, the sun was tipping the treetops with greeny-gold.

While still in her sleeping bag, she wriggled into her clothes. Then she squirmed out, picking up her sneakers as she left the tent. Peter was already up.

"I found an orange and some cinnamon rolls," he whispered.

Megan tied her sneaker laces. "What about something to drink?" She lifted the lid of the ice chest. "Here are some juice boxes."

She put them into the bag with the other food.

Peter climbed over the big log ahead of her and reached for the bag. "Want me to carry that?"

"I've got it. Go ahead."

The distant Olympics poked sharp peaks through fog rolling across the Strait of Juan de Fuca, but sunlight warmed the bluff where they walked.

"Here's the trail," Peter whispered. Making no sound, he slipped through the bushes and stepped onto the log. A silver film of dew made the footing slick. He teetered down its length, Megan close behind, then crept along the twisting path.

A twig cracked under his foot. "Rats!" he muttered. Another step and they reached the edge of the clearing and the hollow beneath the fallen tree.

Over Peter's shoulder, Megan's gaze met the dark, almond-shaped eyes of the garbage can boy. Wrapped in his blanket, he raised up on one elbow, the dirty baseball cap askew over his face.

Before Megan or Peter could speak, he flung the

blanket aside, leaped from his bed of evergreen branches, and darted into the woods.

Megan dropped the bag of food. She and Peter scrambled under the downed tree and after the barefoot boy. His dash took him straight into a patch of thorny wild rosebushes.

"Stop," Peter yelled, but the boy dodged. Peter launched himself through the air, catching him around the waist. They both crashed to the ground. The boy's cap flew off. He struggled and kicked as Peter pinned both arms to the ground. Then he burst into sobs.

"Hey, don't cry. We aren't going to hurt you." Peter held on to one skinny arm as he helped the box sit up. "We brought you some food."

The boy lifted his head and tossed stringy black hair out of terrified eyes. Though smaller than either Peter or Megan, he seemed to be about the same age. Under the dirt, his skin was smooth and golden, his cheekbones high.

Megan took a closer look. "Peter," she said. "Peter, this isn't a boy."

The ragged person took a deep breath, gulped back a sob, and glared at them. "So what if I'm not a boy? Does that give you a right to chase me and tackle me like you're some kind of ... of ... football player?"

Peter's face turned red. "I'm sorry. We just wanted to help you."

"I'm Megan Parnell," Megan said. "This is my step-brother, Peter Lewis."

"We're camping here," Peter added. "Are you hurt?"

The girl sniffed and rubbed her shoulder. She

picked a thorn from one of her scratched ankles. "I guess not. Did you say you brought some food?"

"Yes," Megan said. "I dropped it in your camp."

They went back to her hideout. While the girl put on her sneakers, Megan opened the bag. They sat in silence while the thin girl devoured three cinnamon rolls, an orange, and all the juice they'd brought.

"How long since you've had a decent meal?" Megan asked when she finished.

"And why are you here, all by yourself?" questioned Peter.

The girl stared at them, as if wondering how much she could trust them. Then, making her decision, she began to talk.

"My name is Thuy Nguyen."

"Twee Newen?" repeated Peter.

She nodded. "My family came from Vietnam ... not me, I was born here ... But my brother was born in a refugee camp. We live in Madrona Bay now."

"Madrona Bay!" Megan said. "That's where we live. Where do you go to school?"

"Madrona Bay High."

"We go there too! But what are you doing here?"

"I'm waiting." Thuy glanced around nervously. "You won't tell the park ranger about me, will you?"

"Not if you don't want us to," Peter answered. "Who are you waiting for?"

"My brother."

"Where is he?"

Thuy's face crumpled. "I don't know," she wailed. "I don't know where I am, either."

Megan and Peter looked at each other.

"Start at the beginning," Megan suggested. "None of this makes any sense."

"All right," Thuy agreed. "My parents were refugees. My mother died several years ago."

She paused. "My father had been a shopkeeper in Vietnam, but when he and mother and Dinh and our grandmother came to this country, he worked for some fishermen who owned a big boat. After a while he bought himself a smaller boat."

Tears came to Thuy's eyes. She told how her father had become ill and died just before school ended last spring. "Dinh's 17. He has a summer job at a grocery store, but that's not enough money for all of us. So on weekends he and I take my father's boat and catch fish or crab. We use what we need and our neighbors buy anything extra we catch."

"You were fishing?" asked Peter. "That's how you got here?"

"Yes. Sunday we stopped at a town called Coupeville to buy some supplies and ... and ..."

"That's almost a week ago," Megan cried. "What happened?"

"We tied our boat to a float and climbed up to the wharf. Other boats were tied there. Some of the owners were at one end of the wharf drinking. A couple of men watched us ... some people don't like Vietnamese fishermen. They say we don't follow the rules. But Dinh and I do ... so did our father.

"Anyway ..." Thuy gulped and wiped away a tear, "while we were in the store, those men cut our boat loose. When we came back, we saw our boat drifting away. We tried to run down to the float. But the men blocked our way. When Dinh tried to get past them, they started to push him around and hit him. Dinh shouted at me to run."

Thuy looked down at her scratched and dirty hands, then up at Megan and Peter. "I'm ashamed to say I did ... I was so frightened. I ran down the wharf all the way to the street. I jumped into the first hiding place I saw, the back of a pickup truck.

"But the truck wasn't parked. It had just paused at a crosswalk, and before I knew what was happening, it drove away. It didn't stop until it came to this place. Then I jumped out ... and found this spot to hide and wait for Dinh. Oh, I hope those men didn't hurt him!"

"But, Thuy," Peter said, "Fort Ebey must be four or five miles from Coupeville! How would Dinh know where to find you?"

Thuy looked miserable. "I didn't know what else to do. I was afraid I might get in trouble for stealing a ride in that truck, or for camping here without paying. Then Dinh and I might never find each other!"

"Oh, Thuy. The park rangers would have helped you," Megan said. "We'll help too, won't we, Peter?"

"Sure," he answered. "The first thing to do is find out what happened to Dinh. He probably went home, don't you think?"

"Maybe. You'll really help me?" Thuy's dirty face lit up. "I'm sorry that I scared you in the bunker yesterday."

"That was you?" Megan asked.

"Yes. I heard you coming and ran in there to hide. I was so frightened when your dog barked."

She shook the fir needles from the blanket and began to fold it. "I borrowed this blanket from somebody's campsite. I can give it back now." She pulled a denim knapsack from a hiding spot under the tree, slung it over one shoulder, and took a final look around.

Megan thought of another question as they stepped onto the path to the campground. "Thuy, last night Peter and I heard somebody playing a flute. Did you hear it too?"

Thuy smiled. "Yes, I heard it." She patted a bulge in her knapsack. "It was me."

~~~~~~~~~~~~~~~~~~~~~~~~~~~

The aroma of coffee and frying bacon floated to meet them as Megan and Peter led Thuy into their campsite. Darren Lewis walked into camp from the other direction with Jiggs on his leash. He stopped, staring at the ragged, dirty girl, and his face went pale. Megan's mom turned from the picnic table. She studied Thuy in amazement.

Jiggs strained ahead, tail wagging. Thuy shrank behind the other two. Megan put an arm around her. "The dog is Jiggs. He's friendly. Everybody, this is Thuy Nguyen."

Sarah's smile welcomed the girl. "Hello, Thuy," she said. "Would you like to join us for breakfast?"

"Th ... thank you."

Peter grabbed a couple of towels and washcloths from the clothesline strung between two trees. "I need to wash my hands and face. How about you, Thuy? I'll show you where the washrooms are."

When Peter and Thuy were out of hearing, Sarah turned to her husband and asked, "Are you all right?"

He nodded, still pale. "I'm fine."

Megan filled them in on Thuy's story. Darren listened, the expression on his face unreadable. Suddenly Megan remembered—he'd received the injury that made him limp in Vietnam. Would that affect his willingness to help Thuy?

"Why, the poor child!" Sarah exclaimed as Megan finished. "Her family must be worried to death!"

"Seeing her come out of the brush like that—I saw ragged, abandoned kids like that in Nam—" Darren shook his head as if to clear the memory. "We could call her grandmother from the ranger's office," he said.

Megan let out her breath. "Or I could drive her to Coupeville to use a telephone," she offered. "Then if her brother's alerted the police, we can tell them that Thuy is safe."

"I suppose you could do that," Darren said.

When Thuy returned, a good deal of the grime had disappeared from her face and hands. "I saw showers in the washroom," Thuy said. "But they take money."

"We've got lots of quarters," Megan said. "And I have extra clean clothes."

"Fine," said Mom. "But breakfast first. Are you hungry, Thuy?"

"Megan and Peter already gave me food," she said. "But I'd be happy to sit down with you."

They all sat down and joined hands around the

table. Thuy looked surprised, but when they bowed their heads, she bowed hers too.

"Heavenly Father," prayed Peter's father, "thank You for protecting Thuy through this long and difficult week. We ask that her family will soon be reunited. And thank You for this wonderful breakfast. In Jesus' name. Amen."

"Amen!" Peter agreed. Sarah handed him a platter of bacon and eggs. He took two eggs and some bacon, then passed the platter to Thuy. She looked at his plate, then put the same amount of food on hers.

The toast came by. He took several slices. So did Thuy. He helped himself from a plate of melon. Thuy did too.

As she demolished the food piled on her plate, Megan tried not to stare. Thuy held out her cup to be refilled with cocoa. "Thank you," she said. "I was very hungry."

After her second breakfast, Thuy showered. Megan gave her one of her own oversized tops and a pair of striped shorts, which Thuy bunched around her slender middle and held in place with a rope belt. When her hair dried, it hung thick and glossy in a pixie cut around her face.

"Our parents say I can drive you back to Coupeville to call your grandmother," Megan told her.

"Oh, good. Dinh's probably home, like you said. I know they'll be worried about me."

"Tell Dinh and the grandmother that we will bring Thuy home," said Darren Lewis. "Come and get your mom and me first, Megan, then we'll drive back to the

Clinton-Mukilteo ferry. If they can meet her on the Mukilteo side we won't have to pay fare for the vehicle. We'll just walk her over. Peter, why don't you go with the girls."

As Megan drove them out of the park, Peter and Thuy talked about the classes they'd signed up for in school. Thuy said she planned to join the school orchestra.

Megan thought about Thuy hiding at Fort Ebey for almost a week. Were the police searching for her? Surely the parks were one of the first places they'd make inquiries. Near the park entrance she saw a ranger cutting brush around a sign. The ranger could tell them if the police had asked about Thuy. She stopped the van and leaned out the window.

"Excuse me," she called.

As the ranger walked over to them, Megan glanced at Thuy. She looked scared. Quickly Megan rephrased the question she wanted to ask.

"We're looking for a 17-year-old boy named Dinh Nguyen. He's my friend's brother. Have you seen him?"

The woman shook her head. "Sorry. Haven't met anyone by that name."

Thuy bit her lip. Megan drove on toward Coupeville, turning left where a pedestrian overpass crossed the north-south highway. Cresting a hill, they found themselves looking down on the town of Coupeville and the quiet waters of Penn Cove.

They passed an old-fashioned church with fancy woodwork and a steeple and several beautifully restored Victorian-style homes. Some had Bed-and-Breakfast signs out front.

Front Street ran along a bluff above the water. They turned left and drove along the short street, past some false-fronted shops which probably looked much as they had in the 1880s.

"Anybody see a pay phone?" Megan asked.

"There's one," Peter said. He pointed to a telephone on the outside of a building. Trees shaded benches near it, and behind them, a wharf jutted into Penn Cove.

"This is it," Thuy cried. "This is the place it happened!"

Megan parked. She looped the strap of her camera around her neck as they walked a few steps onto the wharf. At the far end, white letters on a red building said Harbor Store.

She leaned over the railing. Low tide exposed mussels and barnacles clinging to the pilings. Beside the Harbor Store, a walkway slanted down to docking floats. Small boats snuggled against them.

"See your boat?" Peter asked Thuy.

"No." Anxiety shadowed her face.

"Dinh probably got it back and took it home when he couldn't find you," Megan reassured her. She dug in her pocket for quarters. "Here's money for the phone."

"Thank you."

Thuy dropped a quarter in the slot and dialed. Her face lit up as someone answered. She put more money in the phone and began to talk rapidly in Vietnamese. The others caught their own names, then Dinh's.

Suddenly Thuy's eyes widened. Her face grew pale. She sagged against the phone booth as she listened to her grandmother. She spoke into the phone again, then held the receiver against her chest.

"My grandmother is crying. She is happy that I am safe. But Dinh ... Dinh has not come home."

Megan and Peter stared at Thuy. She looked small and forlorn as she clutched the phone to her chest.

"Tell your grandmother we'll try to find your brother," Megan said. "Tell her you'll call back."

Thuy spoke into the phone again. She hung up and looked at them despairingly. "Dinh would have called Grandmother if he was all right. Maybe those men killed him!"

"They wouldn't have dared ... especially with other people on the wharf," Megan comforted her.

"There's got to be some other explanation," said Peter.

"Yes," Megan said. "I think the first thing we should do is try to find somebody who saw what happened." They walked down the long wharf, passing several tourists strolling along with soft drinks in their hands.

When they reached the building at the end of the wharf, Thuy pointed to one of the floats. "We tied our boat there," she said. "The floats were higher though. The tide was just turning."

Narrow Penn Cove stretched eastward to Saratoga Passage, which separated Whidbey from Camano Island. Megan didn't say anything, but even a landlubber could see that if the tide took the Nguyen's boat out of Penn Cove it might be lost for good. She hoped Dinh had been able to retrieve it.

A couple of people sat outdoors at a table in a roped-off area behind the Harbor Store, drinking coffee. "Many people were sitting there Sunday. They were very noisy," said Thuy.

"Let's see if anyone in the store knows anything," Peter suggested.

They went into the almost-deserted souvenir shop/restaurant inside the building. A stairway led to more tables in an open loft. Behind a counter, a man slapped sandwiches together. He looked up. "Hi. What can I do for you?"

"We hope you can give us some information," Megan answered. "Were you working here last Sunday?"

"No. Why?"

"This is our friend, Thuy Nguyen. She and her brother tied up to the wharf that day. Some men cut their boat adrift and beat up her brother. They got separated, and she hasn't seen him since. We're looking for someone who might have seen what happened."

"Do you live on the island?" the man asked Thuy.

"No. We're from Madrona Bay. Dinh never came home."

The man looked as if he wasn't sure he believed the story, but he called to a young woman descending the stairs with a tray of dishes. "Hey, Jen, you worked Sunday. Talk to these kids, would you?"

They repeated the story to the waitress.

"There *was* some kind of ruckus outside, but I was

busy in here," she said. "I remember some customers came in, upset about some drunken bullies. One said he'd told them to leave or he'd call the police."

"Did they go?" Megan asked.

"I guess they did. I didn't hear anything more."

"Did the customers say what happened to my brother?" Thuy asked eagerly.

"No, honey. I'm sorry."

The light in Thuy's eyes dimmed. "Thank you anyway."

They turned to go.

"Hey, kids. Just a minute." They turned back to the waitress. "I know the girl who cashiers on Saturdays and Sundays. I'll call and see if she knows anything, if you like."

"Oh, great," Peter said. "Would you?"

"Sure. I've got a brother myself," Jen grinned at Peter. "He looks a lot like you."

Soon Jen came back. "Lisa saw a part of it through the door. Said she saw a young boy ... must have meant you, honey," Jen said to Thuy, "... a boy dash past the door and toward the street. She heard the customers threaten to call the police."

"Did she say anything about Dinh?" Peter interrupted anxiously.

"She saw an older Vietnamese boy, about 16 or 17 years old, stagger against the railing and stand there for a few minutes. Looked kind of dazed. Then he started down the wharf toward shore. She figured he was okay."

Thuy let out a big sigh. "Then he's still alive."

They thanked the waitress and stepped outside to

think about their next move. A sea gull flew onto a float below them and dropped a sea urchin at the feet of its mate.

"Look at that!" Peter said.

The gull picked up the urchin and dropped it again and again until the shell cracked. The two gulls, sunshine glinting off their snowy heads and breasts, took turns poking yellow beaks into the contents of the shell. "Gross," Peter said. "I wouldn't want that for breakfast."

Megan lifted her camera and snapped a picture. "Wish I had a telephoto lens," she said.

"What should we do now?" Thuy asked.

"It might not help," said Peter, "but we could ask in the shops if anyone saw Dinh."

"It's worth a try. Let's split up," Megan suggested. "Peter, do you want to take the water side of the street? Thuy and I can take the other."

They separated at the end of the wharf. Megan and Thuy dodged between cars and headed for the minimall housed in an old building across the street.

They made the rounds of the shops in the minimall without success. In an office marked Ebey's Landing National Historical Reserve, Megan picked some brochures from a rack. She scanned one of them. "This looks interesting," she remarked. "It says that where we're camping is part of the Reserve. So is this town."

"I don't want to look at tourist brochures right now," Thuy answered impatiently. "We need to look for Dinh."

"Okay. Let's go on up the street. He must have stopped *somewhere* searching for you."

When they met Peter coming out of the last shop, they knew without asking that he had no news to share either.

"We're parked in front of the museum," Megan said. "Let's check there first. If they can't help, we can ask where the police station is and report Dinh missing."

Thuy's eyes widened in fear.

"It's all right," Peter said to her. "Police officers help find missing people all the time."

A lady at the museum gave them directions to the marshal's office across the street from the Island County Courthouse, a few blocks up the hill. They talked to an officer who listened carefully.

"I have no information about the incident," he told them. "Since none of you are of legal age, I'll have to ask you to bring in an adult to file an official report. Then we'll see what we can do."

Back at the van, Peter fumed. "This is just wasting time. Why wouldn't he believe us?"

"He probably believed us," Megan said. "But he has to follow the rules."

"I didn't think the police would help anyway," said Thuy in a dejected voice.

"They'll do all they can, Thuy. We'll get my mom or Peter's dad to come talk to them." They piled back into the Dodge Caravan. As she drove back to Fort Ebey, Megan wished there was some other way they could help Thuy. Suddenly an idea popped into her head.

"Everybody, listen!" She slowed and glanced at Peter and Thuy. "The waitress saw Dinh walk along the wharf toward town. That means he probably *didn't* go after your boat, Thuy. Why don't we ask if we can take our boat and see if yours went ashore somewhere in Penn Cove? After we talk to the marshal again, of course."

~~~~~~~~~~~~~~~~~~~~

When the three young people reported back to camp, the adults decided that Darren Lewis would return with them to Coupeville to talk to the marshall then go with them to search for the missing boat. Megan's mom would drive the van north to Oak Harbor, asking along the way for news of Dinh.

"Why don't we make posters to put in stores and on telephone poles?" Megan suggested. "Mom could take some along with her."

"Yeah! We could probably find a copy machine in Coupeville," Peter said. "What's the name of your boat, Thuy? We could ask people if they've seen it too."

"It's called the Good Fortune. It looks like this."

Thuy picked up a twig and in the dirt she sketched a picture of a slender vessel with a low cabin. "It's gray, with a white cabin."

Megan crawled into her tent and came back with a couple sheets of paper from her sketchbook. "Here, draw it on one of these."

"Should we have people call the marshal if they see the boat or Dinh?" asked Peter.

Thuy looked up from her sketching. "If we put that on here, and Dinh reads the poster, he might think he's in trouble because of the fight on the wharf."

"I know," said Peter. "We can say, 'Dinh Nguyen, your sister is looking for you.' Then he won't be afraid."

He wrote the words across the top of the page. Below them, he printed: *Missing: Dinh Nguyen and his vessel, Good Fortune. Last seen at Coupeville wharf. If anyone has seen Dinh or the boat, please call _____.* He left space for the marshal's phone number and for Thuy's drawing.

While Thuy worked on the sketch of the Good Fortune, Peter helped his dad hitch the boat to the pickup. Jiggs pranced and wagged his tail.

"Jiggs, you'd better come with me," Sarah Lewis said, opening the door of the van for him. "They don't need you in the boat."

Everybody drove first to Coupeville, where the girls made copies of the poster while Peter bought thumbtacks and tape to put them up. Sarah Lewis took some copies to give out on her drive north. "You all be careful," she said. "I'll meet you back at Fort Ebey."

Darren Lewis made the official missing persons report at the marshal's office then drove to the community boat launch at the edge of town. The three young people hopped out while he backed the boat trailer down the concrete ramp. When the boat floated, Peter grabbed a rope attached to the bow and held it while his father pulled the trailer ahead and parked.

Megan tacked a poster to a piling next to the launch ramp. Peter and Thuy climbed up on some broken chunks of concrete beside her. They looked back at the wharf with its many pilings and the red, warehouse-like building on the end.

"I lost my mother and my father. Now I've lost my brother," Thuy said softly.

"You haven't lost him," Peter said. "We'll find him."

"How can you be so sure?"

"Well ... we asked God to help us, remember? And we know Dinh got away from those men." He smiled. "Your boat may be named 'Good Fortune,' but your fortune isn't so good right now. We believe good blessings come from God. He'll help us."

Thuy was silent for a moment. "I'm glad you and Megan found me." She smiled a small, shy smile at him.

"Me too," Peter said. He jumped down and held up a hand to Thuy.

He's really a nice guy, Megan thought, watching Peter encourage Thuy. She smiled to herself. From the way Thuy looked at him, it seemed Thuy thought so too.

"Let's go," Darren called from the boat. Peter held the boat steady while the girls scrambled in, then gave it a shove and hopped in himself. His father started the motor.

To their right, the beach curved in, then out, below a bluff topped with houses. They saw only a few boats drawn up along the beach. They rounded the point and followed the shoreline.

Far across Penn Cove, fields and forest crowned tall sandy cliffs. Sea gulls wheeled overhead, and a jet or two traced sky-trails across heavens as blue as the water.

"Do you think the Good Fortune could have floated all the way over there?" Megan asked, gesturing toward the far side of the cove.

"Not likely if the current was strong," answered Peter. Closer at hand, rowboats bobbed at the foot of bluff-front property, and cabin cruisers floated at anchor. But they saw no slim gray fishing boat.

"Was there a breeze the day you stopped at Coupeville, Thuy?" Darren Lewis shouted above the noise of the motor.

"Maybe a little one. About like today," she called back.

"Why do you ask?" Megan inquired.

"Wind would affect where the boat might drift."

They glided along a beach tossed with silver driftwood, but no gray hull lay among it. Near a point where summer houses crowded the bottom of the bluff, a sign warned "Private Beach."

"That," Megan said, "shouldn't be allowed. Nice beaches like that should belong to everybody!"

"There's a gray boat over there."

Peter indicated one of the pleasure craft tied to a floating dock.

"It's not the Good Fortune," Thuy said.

"This is the mouth of Penn's Cove," Darren Lewis said as they rounded the point. "The current could have taken it anywhere from here. We'd better go back."

"Can't we go as far as that next point jutting out there to the south?" Peter asked.

His father looked at Thuy's anxious face. "Okay, but no farther. That's the only place left to look without a major, time-consuming search. We'd have to get more help."

They followed the beach down-island to where it curved out to the spot Peter had indicated. Ahead, children were clambering over driftwood logs. "I don't see anything," said Megan, shading her eyes to look far down the beach.

As their motorboat neared the children, a little boy waved from atop the roots of an immense upended stump near the water's edge, then disappeared behind the spreading roots. They saw more logs scattered along the shore. Maybe the boat had sunk, Megan thought.

"Oh!" Thuy gasped as the boy reappeared behind the stump on what at first seemed to be just another log. "There it is! That's it!"

Darren Lewis switched off the engine and let the motorboat coast to shore. As the bottom slid along the gravel, Megan, Peter, and Thuy kicked off their shoes and jumped into the shallow water. The children popped out of the boat's cabin, looking puzzled and a bit frightened as the three raced toward them.

"It's the Good Fortune all right, Thuy." Peter touched the oriental-style red letters which spelled the words.

"It is!" Thuy half laughed, half cried. "Is it hurt?"

They circled the graceful little craft, searching the hull for damage.

"All I see is some scratched paint," Peter said.

"This is *our* boat," a small boy challenged. "We found it."

"It really belongs to our friend Thuy and her brother," Megan told him. She picked up the end of a rope which dangled from the bow. "See? Some bad men cut this rope loose from the dock at Coupeville, so the boat floated away from them."

"Is there a red jacket hanging in the cabin?" asked Thuy. The children nodded. "That's mine," she said.

"There's some crab pots in the hold. Want me to show you?"

"We saw them," the little boy said. "Okay, it's your boat. We didn't hurt anything. We were just pretending to be fishermen."

He and the other children climbed over the side and watched as Peter inspected the hull.

His father beckoned Megan off to the side. "You were smart to bring your camera, Megan. How about taking some snapshots? They might be valuable if this should come to a lawsuit."

Megan glanced at Thuy and lowered her voice. "You mean, if we don't find Dinh?"

"One never knows," he said. "You kids have certainly uncovered a mystery here."

Megan thought about his words as she snapped pictures from every angle. How Dinh could so completely disappear really *was* mysterious.

"The tide wedged the Good Fortune against the driftwood just right to keep it upright," said Peter. "Evidently the tide's not been high enough since then to wash it away again."

"We should be able to get it afloat with all of us to help," his father said. He and Peter pulled on the dangling rope. The girls pushed. The children lent their efforts at the stern. With a great deal of puffing and grunting, they finally got the Good Fortune into water deep enough to float it. The children cheered.

"We'll check it again for leaks when we get it back to the dock," said Darren.

Peter splashed over to the motorboat for a length of

rope. He tied the two boats together.

Some time later they drew up alongside one of the floats at the Coupeville wharf and made the Good Fortune secure. Peter's dad checked below deck to be sure no water had come in.

"All tight," he said. "You girls want to stay here while Peter and I go back to the boat launch? We'll load our boat on the trailer and stop to tell the marshal we found the Good Fortune. We can meet you in front of the museum."

"Okay," Megan said. The boat's motor surged. Megan watched Peter and his father skim away. This camping trip had turned out to be anything but boring! "Did you and Dinh really stay all night on this little boat, Thuy?" she asked. "It looks so small."

"Most nights we went home to stay with Grandmother," Thuy answered. "But it's not really so small. Would you like to see?"

Megan followed as she hopped aboard the Good Fortune. Thuy showed her the neat cabin with bunks, storage cupboards, and a tiny galley. While Megan looked around, the other girl pulled some of her clothing from a cupboard and stuffed it into a bag to take with her. Megan noticed her red rain jacket hanging on a hook next to Dinh's larger rain gear.

On deck, Thuy lifted a hatch to show her the crab pots. "Everything's here," Thuy said. A shadow crossed her face.

Everything but Dinh, Megan thought. When and where would Thuy find her brother again?

Disappointment
at Fort Casey

Thuy picked up her knapsack. Megan watched her touch the bulge of her flute as if seeking reassurance from an old friend. She followed Thuy up the ramp.

Halfway along the wharf, a browned and muscular young man leaned against the rail, fishing. Megan's hand automatically patted her tousled hair into place. As they came closer, she noticed a net bag full of blue-black mussels at his feet, dribbling water across the planks.

"Wonder what he's doing with those?" Megan whispered to Thuy.

He heard her. His glance traveled from the bag of shellfish, up Megan's long tanned legs, up to her face. An admiring grin crinkled his eyes and creased his lean cheeks. "Did you think I'm fishing for mussels? They're bait."

His line jerked, and he reeled in a small but lively fish. "See? Fish love 'em."

Megan smiled back. "Do you live here in Coupeville?" she asked.

"Yes."

He slid the fish off the hook and leaned over the rail to drop it back into the water. "I'm a custodian evenings.

Fish and loaf all day. Haven't seen you girls before. Just visiting?"

Megan nodded.

Thuy looked up, a hopeful glint in her eyes. "Were you here last Sunday?"

"Matter of fact, I was. Why?"

She told him about the fight on the dock.

"Oh, so that's what happened."

"So that's *what* happened?" Megan asked.

"There were lots of people on the dock," he explained. "Kids running back and forth, boats crowding the floats ... I heard shouting by the restaurant. I was over there." He jerked his thumb toward the opposite railing.

"Couldn't see what was happening. I was going to check it out, but the noise stopped so I went back to fishing. Pretty soon this Chinese or Korean guy ..."

"Vietnamese," murmured Thuy.

"Vietnamese? Could be. Anyway ... this guy wandered past, holding his head like he had a terrific headache."

"Was he wearing a blue shirt?" Thuy cried.

The young man frowned, trying to remember. "I think it *was* blue."

"Dinh wore a blue shirt," Megan said. "What did he do then?"

"Nothing, at first," the fisherman said. "He sat on one of those benches at the end of the wharf with his head in his hands for a long time. I was about to go see if he was okay when some people came along. They talked to him for a while. Then he got up and went with them ... got into their van and they drove away."

"I know it was Dinh," cried Thuy. "But why didn't he look for me? Did you see where they went?"

"Up the hill." The fisherman shrugged. "The van was old, brown ... needed body work and paint."

Good, Megan thought. The van is the first solid clue we've had, besides finding the Good Fortune. "What make was the van? A Volkswagen?"

"Not a VeeDub ... a Ford, I think."

"What did the people look like?"

"You sure ask a lot of questions."

The young man smiled at Megan's eagerness. He thought a moment. "One was a girl ... jeans, brown hair in a braid. And a man in his 20's, skinny, tall ... very ordinary looking."

He reached down to take a mussel out of the bag and pried the two halves of the shell apart with his jack-knife. "Sorry I can't do more to help you find your friend. I'd be glad to show you how to catch fish with mussels."

"We're meeting somebody soon," Megan told him. "But you've been a great help. Thank you."

As they reached the end of the wharf and the benches where Dinh had last been seen, Thuy struggled without success to hold back tears. Megan put her arm around the other girl's shoulders. "He gave us a good lead, Thuy. That van should be easy to find, especially if it belongs to somebody on the island."

"Yes." Thuy nodded and tried to smile.

They looked up and down the street. "Peter and Darren aren't here yet," said Megan. "Shall we browse in that bookstore over there? We can ask the owners if they know a van like that."

"All right."

They stopped in front of the bookshop to look at the display in the window. "Those are beautiful quartz crystals," Thuy said. "Do you think they found them on the island?"

"I don't know," Megan answered. "I've never seen anything but plain old gravel and rocks here."

She noted the covers of the books in the window. *Cosmic Vibrations. Raise Your Consciousness with Crystals.*

"It must be a Christian bookstore," Thuy said, pointing to one titled *The Power within You.* "That sounds like a religious book."

"They might be religious," Megan said as she followed Thuy into the store. "But I don't think they're Christian books."

The air inside smelled heavy and sweetish. "Incense," Thuy whispered. "My grandmother burns it sometimes."

The shopkeeper, a woman with long crinkly hair and sandals on her stockingless feet, drifted about the room, rearranging books on shelves, and humming along with flute music floating from a stereo. She smiled vaguely in their direction.

Megan leafed through a book about Native American culture and one on taking care of the environment. She skipped over some illustrated children's stories and scanned what appeared to be a fantasy novel. But the author seemed to believe this fantasy.

"Weird," she muttered as her eyes lit on phrases like "worship the goddess" and "Gaia, goddess of the earth." She set the book down and joined Thuy in a corner where tapes and sheet music were displayed.

"Megan, look! Here's the Mozart piece I've been wanting for months!" Regretfully, Thuy replaced it. "I can't buy it. Dinh had all our money."

Megan felt in the pocket of her shorts. "I have three dollars. Is that enough?"

"Oh, thank you!" Thuy's dark eyes lit up. "I'll ask."

The shopkeeper took the three dollars and put the music in a recycled plastic bag. "Mozart's music was so in tune with the Eternal Consciousness, so centered. Don't you agree?"

Thuy nodded politely. They left. Outside the shop, Megan said, "I'm glad we found the music you wanted, Thuy."

"Me too. But there's something odd about that place. What was that woman talking about?"

"Some kind of New Age stuff, I guess," answered Megan. She glanced down the street. "Oh, the guys are back. There's the truck and boat in front of the museum."

While the girls repeated the fisherman's story, Darren Lewis listened thoughtfully. "Whoever owned the van may live nearby. We'd better tell the marshal what you learned. If the van's not local, he may want to bring the Island County sheriff into the case.

"But first, Thuy," he suggested, "why don't you call your grandmother again? See if she's heard from Dinh. If she's worried about you, we can take you home right away."

Take Thuy home before finding Dinh? Oh no, thought Megan. That would be worse than reading only half of a good book and never knowing how it ended! They all walked the few steps over to the phone by the wharf and waited while Thuy made the call.

"What did she say?" Peter asked when Thuy hung up.

"Dinh hasn't come home or called. She asked about you and I told her you were all really kind and are taking good care of me."

"How is she holding up?" Darren asked.

"She's terribly worried about Dinh," Thuy answered. "She's going to get a neighbor to take her to the police station to file a missing person report, but she says I can stay with you and keep looking. That is, if you don't mind my spoiling your vacation plans."

"You're not spoiling anything, young lady," Darren answered heartily. "We want to help. Don't we, gang?"

Darren seemed to be assuming leadership. Sudden resentment welled in Megan. After all, this was *her* mystery to solve ... hers and Thuy's ... and Peter's. Then she felt ashamed. They needed all the help they could get.

"Sure," Peter said to Thuy. "We want to find Dinh too. But first, let's get the rest of our posters up, then get something to eat. I'm starved."

While Darren Lewis walked to the marshal's office, the girls and Peter asked permission to leave fliers in some of the shops along Front Street. They also asked about the brown van and its passengers, with no luck. When they finished, they returned to the truck.

"Maybe they stopped to get gas while they were here," Megan mused, still thinking about the van. "I wonder if there are any gas stations or repair shops in town?"

"I saw one near the main highway," Peter replied.

While they waited for Peter's dad, they wandered over to look at some Indian dugout canoes displayed under a pole shelter near the museum.

"What a lot of work went into these!" Megan exclaimed, reaching up to touch the biggest canoe, blackened and split with age. "Look at these thousands of chisel marks."

"What is this for?" A few steps away, Thuy peeked through the doorway of a log building. It's like two small windowless rooms stacked one atop the other. The top room was larger and overhung the lower.

"It's a blockhouse," Peter said. "See the gun slits up near the top?"

"The settlers built blockhouses for defense against hostile Indians," Megan told her.

"I've heard of blockhouses, of course. You mean there were Indian battles right here?"

"None that I know of. The Indians who lived here got along pretty well with the whites," she said. "But both the local Indians and the settlers were afraid of Indian raiders from Canada and their big war canoes."

She patted the pocket with the brochures she'd picked up that morning. "That's how Captain Ebey was beheaded."

"Beheaded? What kind of story is that?" Peter's face mirrored his disbelief, but before he could say any more, they saw his dad coming down the street with his hands full of ice-cream cones. They forgot the subject of

Captain Ebey's head.

"The ice cream's to hold you until we get back to camp," Darren told them as they climbed into the truck. "The marshal doesn't know anyone with a van like you described. Did you find out anything?"

"No," Peter answered, catching the drips from his cone with his tongue.

"Well, maybe they trade at one of the local garages or gas stations. We can check on our way out of town," Darren said.

That was *my* idea, Megan thought. Peter and Thuy were both too busy with their ice cream to give her credit, so she said nothing.

No one at the repair shop or the gas stations they stopped at could help, so they drove back to camp. Sarah was packing fried chicken into a picnic basket under Jiggs' watchful scrutiny.

"I stopped at every place of business along the road to Oak Harbor, asking questions and leaving your fliers," she said. "Nobody knew anything."

She closed the lid of the basket and put her arm around Thuy. "How did your morning go?"

Thuy told her about finding the boat and repeated the fisherman's story.

"Well, that's good news! We'll find Dinh," Sarah said. "We'll just keep looking. Can we all fit into the van?"

"Sure," said her husband. "What do you have in mind?"

"Let's drive over to Fort Casey for lunch. The kids might like to explore the fortifications. And the Keystone ferry landing is right there. That's a logical place to inquire after Dinh."

"Good idea!" Megan said. "May I drive?"

Sarah's eyes met her husband's, but she spoke to Megan. "Don't you think so many passengers might be distracting, Meg?"

Megan had asked her mother. Why did Mom need to consult Darren? "Passengers don't bother me." She tried to appear nonchalant, but the words came out sounding brash and overconfident. She caught Peter's sharp glance and tossed her head. He's just jealous, she thought, and added, "I'll drive slowly."

Sarah nodded. "All right. Go ahead."

Peter, Thuy, and Darren climbed into the back of the van with Jiggs, who poked his head out the open window. Her mom settled herself in the front passenger's seat, and Megan got behind the wheel. She started the engine, more nervous than she wanted to admit, and soon they were rolling down-island again.

"Turn right," Sarah said when they reached the Coupeville intersection.

"I know, Mom. Remember, you and I drove this way last time we were on the island."

Farmers were harvesting corn and potatoes in the sweeping fields along the road. To the west, the rich farmland ended in bluffs like the ones at Fort Ebey. Beyond the bluffs, the Strait of Juan de Fuca sparkled in the sun.

"What a view!" exclaimed Peter.

"Most of this was Isaac Ebey's claim," Megan's mother said. "It's called Ebey's Prairie."

"The same Ebey who lost his head?" Peter asked.

Sarah nodded yes.

Megan added, "I read that before Ebey and the other settlers ever came, the Indians cleared and cultivated these prairies."

"This soil looks like it would grow anything," Darren said.

"My brother loves to work with the soil," Thuy commented. "He made a little garden for my grandmother behind our apartment."

In the rearview mirror, Megan saw Thuy stare hard at some field workers, then settle back with a disappointed sigh. She drove on past the prairie and through forested uplands, watching for a brown van or anyone who could possibly be Dinh. Then the road curved downhill to a strip of land between the Strait and a marshy lake. Between them and the dark blue salt water, barracks lined one side of a manicured field, fancier buildings the other.

Megan's mother turned to the passengers in the back. "The field is Camp Casey's old parade ground," she said. "Soldiers lived in the barracks, officers in those Victorian houses. This part is used year round for sports camps and retreats."

Just past the barracks, signs directed them straight ahead to the Keystone Ferry or to Fort Casey State Park on the right. They turned up a hill into the park. Megan pulled into a shady picnic area and turned off the engine. Mom had been right. She wasn't used to so many passengers. Her neck felt stiff from tension she hadn't realized was there.

"Eat first, then explore. Okay?" Sarah asked.

Peter's stomach rumbled loudly enough for everyone to hear. "I could eat an elephant," he exclaimed as he pulled the picnic basket from the back of the minivan.

Peter, Megan, and Thuy loaded their plates with potato salad and fried chicken, then sat down on the grass under a tree. A picture flashed into Megan's mind ... another picnic, long ago ... her own father, her mother, and herself sitting on the grass in a park like this and laughing. Her thoughts swirled. If Mom had just been more willing to travel with her dad on his trips overseas, maybe they'd still be a family. No, it was her father who'd insisted Mom stay home and take care of Megan—but maybe, if Mom had tried harder, he'd have wanted to stay with them. Or maybe it was Megan's fault; Mom could have gone with Dad if it hadn't been for her. Suddenly she just wanted to hurt someone.

Peter and Thuy were laughing about something. Peter pulled a bit of crisp skin from his drumstick and tossed it to Jiggs. "This chicken's delicious. Your mom's a great cook, Megan!"

Megan's lip curled. "She didn't cook this. She bought it at a delicatessen this morning."

She saw Peter redden, but a mean little spirit seemed to control her tongue. "Can't you tell deli chicken when you eat it?"

Peter tried to make a joke. "Oh ... well, she's a great shopper, then."

Thuy glanced from one to the other. "It tastes wonderful after a whole week of eating other people's scraps," she said diplomatically. "You have all been so good to me." She paused. "But I don't understand why.

I'm not related to you."

A chance to tell Thuy about God! And she had just blown it. But Peter answered, "We're all part of God's family. God loves everybody, and He helps us love and help others."

"The men who beat up Dinh must not feel that way."

"When people don't have God's love in their hearts they can do awful things," Peter said. He shook his head. "We Christians can do pretty awful things too. But God wants us to love even people who hurt us."

Thuy looked startled. Then she frowned. "I hate those men. How can I love them?"

"You can't, by yourself," Peter told her. "But God can help you forgive them."

As Thuy sat thinking, Megan's mom called, "Watermelon for dessert!"

Carrying her plate back to the table, Megan pondered what Peter had just told Thuy. She resented the turn her life had taken, but she knew Peter was right. She couldn't change her feelings by herself. Help me with what I'm feeling, Jesus, she prayed. I feel like my heart's locked up.

~~~~~~~~~~~~~~~~~~

The fortifications at Fort Casey put those at Fort Ebey to shame. Underground concrete chambers, passages, and gun emplacements rimmed the jutting point of land called Admiralty Head. Megan, Peter, and Thuy stood atop the massive concrete fortifications, which were earth-covered on the seaward side and invisible to passing ships, and looked down at an enormous gun. Megan snapped some pictures.

"The sign down there says the original guns were melted down during World War II," Peter said, pointing to an informational kiosk on the grassy field between them and the woods where they had picnicked. "This gun came from a fort in the Philippines. See, it can be raised up to shoot over this embankment where we're standing, then be retracted."

Megan took another look at the gun, then turned her face up to watch a dozen or more kites being flown from the field. They swooped and dived, straining against the strings tethering them to earth. The kites made brilliant, changing designs against a blue so intense it hurt her eyes. Sea gulls traced patterns among them in white and soaring counterpoint. As she framed her shots, she hoped her camera could capture the color and pattern ... it would take Thuy and her flute to capture the poetry of the motion.

Thuy interrupted her concentration. "Come on, Megan! We're going to explore."

Megan followed her and Peter down some steps beside the big gun and along the upper-level walkway where empty chambers gaped. One had an elevator sort of machine with metal cradles, just the shape and size to hold the gun's ammunition. The shells had been brought up from storage rooms on the lower level, obviously.

By the time Megan caught up, the others had crossed a catwalk to one of the free-standing gun towers that looked over the top of the fortifications. "See," said Peter. "They had a gun on a swivel, right here in the middle."

They peered through the long narrow gun slit that ran at eye level around the tiny concrete room. Among the crowd of visitors wandering over the fortifications, Megan picked out her mom and Darren with Jiggs on his leash. Whooping, hollering kids and young people ran in and out of the concrete chambers that stretched all the way to the end of the point.

"Wish we had binoculars," Megan remarked. "We could stand right here and watch for Dinh."

"I don't know why he'd be here," Thuy said. Her eyes widened with a sudden thought. "... unless he's hiding like I was hiding." She paused. "It wouldn't hurt to look, would it?"

"No," Peter said. "Let's go."

They raced back across the catwalk, through the passages beneath the gun emplacements, shouting Dinh's name into dark and echoing chambers until they were hoarse. Finally they reached the end of the part that was open to the public. They walked back across the wide field, scanning kite flyers and groups of picnickers.

They hiked on, to the nearby Admiralty Head lighthouse, and left some of the posters from Thuy's backpack there and some with a park ranger. By this time, the sun had begun its drop toward the horizon. Another day almost gone and no Dinh, Megan thought as they walked back to the fortifications. Then Peter found a makeshift trail leading to the beach. He plunged over the edge of the bluff and went slipping and sliding down. Megan and Thuy followed, placing their feet carefully.

"We've looked and looked," sighed Thuy as they wandered along the edge of the water. "I'm afraid I'll never see my brother again." She picked up a flat stone and tried to skip it across the waves, but it splashed and sank.

"Oh, look what Peter found," Megan said, hoping to distract her.

They saw him down the beach, tugging at a long, water-smoothed slab of driftwood just right for a teeter-totter. Thuy smiled and ran to help him pull it to a log. They laid it across, and each took an end. Peter's end went down and he sat there, stranding a squealing Thuy high in the air. Megan knelt and took a quick shot of them with the sky as background. Still looking through the viewfinder, she saw Thuy freeze and stare up at the bluff. Megan lowered her camera to follow Thuy's gaze. Several people, too far away to see their faces, stood looking out across the water.

"Dinh was wearing a blue shirt like that," Thuy cried.

A slender young man wore the blue shirt. His skin seemed dark; his hair was black. Megan could not tell whether he was Asian.

Peter lowered the teeter-totter. Thuy leaped off and raced along the beach to another trail. "Dinh!" she called. "Dinh, wait!"

But the people on the bluff turned away and disappeared. Megan and Peter followed Thuy. She had scrambled nearly to the top of the trail by the time they reached it. After they hauled themselves up the steep path, they were gasping for breath.

Thuy had run along the bluff to the right but was now coming back. "The ferry landing is that way, but I couldn't see him on that trail. They must have gone somewhere else." She was trembling and panting.

"Take it easy, Thuy," Peter said. "If that was Dinh, we'll find him. Let's split up and follow all the trails."

Thuy darted away. Peter looked at Megan. "I'll try the one that heads back toward the parking area."

"All right. I'll check the field along the gun emplacements."

After a fruitless search of the park, they met at the picnic area where Darren and Sarah were waiting for them. Jiggs barked and wagged his welcome. Tears crept from beneath Thuy's lashes as she told about the young man they'd seen.

"He could have been a tourist just stopping by," said Darren. "But if it was Dinh, there's a chance he's staying at the campground by the ferry landing or even waiting for a ferry. Let's go take a look."

Thuy nodded and smiled through her tears. It took just a few minutes to drive back to the main road and follow it around the base of the hill to the ferry landing. A small campground snuggled between the cove where the ferry came in and the bluffs of Admiralty Head. They drove through slowly, looking for Dinh among the campers.

Darren shook his head. "Well, let's try the ferry landing." He parked the car beside the saltwater lake. They got out and walked across the road to a holding area filled with cars waiting to cross to Port Townsend.

"The ferry's coming," Megan exclaimed. A white and green ferry, smaller than the one they'd ridden earlier, chugged toward them through the calm water. They could make out the name, "Kittitas," above the car deck.

Megan and the others walked up and down the lines of vehicles, trying to see their occupants without appearing to stare. Metal clanked as the ferry docked and the deckhands lowered the ramp. Vehicles poured off the ferry. Around them, the waiting drivers started their engines.

Megan joined Peter and Thuy near the ramp as the gates came down to allow the foot passengers to load.

"Any luck?" questioned Peter.

She shook her head as she watched a large group of walkers start down the ramp to the ferry. She tensed. One wore a blue shirt. "Thuy, is that him?"

The black-haired young man in the blue shirt was already halfway down the ramp. Thuy gasped, slipped under the gates, and dashed after him. She caught up and grasped the man's arm. He turned. He was in his late 20's, at least, and not Asian. Thuy let go and backed away, then stared after him, the picture of dejection, as the man hurried onto the ferry.

Megan blinked frustrated tears from her own eyes. While they'd been searching for Dinh, the sun had slid behind the Olympic Mountains like a fiery coin slipping into a bank. As the ferry moved out of the inlet, reflections from its lights danced across the ripples toward Megan, Peter, and Thuy. The three sat on the breakwater to watch.

"That's the last trip it will make today," Megan said. Thuy turned her face away.

"We'll keep looking," Peter told her. "Don't get discouraged."

"I'm trying not to."

"Look!" Megan interrupted. "What is it?" She pointed to a strange creature gliding across the entrance to the inlet. Behind the black bulk of its body, a long tail cut through silvery ripples. A graceful neck curved back into the water.

"A dragon!" exclaimed Thuy.

"It's just a log," Peter laughed. "See, the neck is a big crooked root. The tail is a branch trailing behind."

Thuy smiled, although her lip trembled. "I'd rather think it's a dragon. A good-luck dragon to help us find Dinh."

Megan gave her a quick hug and this time she was brave enough to speak up. "Luck won't help. But I'm praying that Jesus will."

The Case
of the Missing Head

The smell of frying bacon edged itself into Megan's dream. She yawned and opened her eyes. Thuy's spot beside her was vacant. Outside the tent, Peter and his father stood listening to distant music floating through the forest. Jiggs kept his attention on the frying pan as Sarah listened while turning the bacon.

Megan poked her head out. "Is that Thuy?"

"Good morning, Megan," Sarah smiled. "Yes. She's been out there for an hour, practicing her new music."

"Why does anyone who can play like that need practice?" Peter commented.

Megan dressed and went to the ladies' room to wash her face and brush the tangles out of her hair. Peter, meanwhile, jogged the campground loop road with Jiggs. The three of them returned to their campsite at the same time.

"I told Thuy we'd call her when breakfast is ready. Would you two like to do that?" Sarah asked.

"Sure." They followed Mozart's music along the edge of the bluff and through the brush to Thuy's old campsite. Thuy perched on the slanting log like an illustration Megan had seen once of Shakespeare's fairy Puck in *A Midsummer Night's Dream.* She'd propped her sheet music in the crook of a branch.

As they came into view, Thuy lowered the flute and smiled. "Hi. Isn't it a beautiful piece?"

"Yes, it is." Peter's admiration was plain to see. "And you make it sound so easy. Did you have to practice a lot to play that well?"

Thuy hopped from the log and put her flute in its case. She gave Jiggs a hug. "Oh, lots. Every serious musician practices hours every day."

"And you are serious?" Megan asked.

"I hope to be a concert musician someday."

"You know," Megan said to Thuy as they walked back to camp, "I think it's great that you work so hard on your music. Not many people our age know what they want to be when they grow up."

She paused, then continued, more to herself than to Thuy. "But I do know that God has a plan for each of us."

Thuy stopped, her eyes widening. "Do you mean God might not want me to play the flute? That He might have a different plan?"

Megan and Peter stopped too. "I didn't mean *that*," Megan said. "He gave you a special gift. He must want you to use it."

Still Thuy didn't move. "Do you think God planned for those men to hurt Dinh?"

Peter answered that one. "No ... but He knows what happened. And He can make bad things work for our good." They turned from the bluff onto the short trail to camp.

"Maybe He is already making a bad thing work out for good," said Thuy. "He brought me four new friends because of those men. Five, counting Jiggs."

~~~~~~~~~~~~~~~~~~~~

"That was the best French toast I ever ate!" Megan said as she rinsed and dried the last plate.

"Didn't you tell me that the last time we had French toast?" her mother teased.

"It's better outdoors. Where's Darren?"

"He went to the Park Ranger's office to use the telephone. He wants to see if the marshal's heard anything before we plan what we'll do today."

Megan carried the dishpan of water to the campground faucet, emptied it into the drain, and rinsed it. Then she joined Thuy and Peter where they sat on the big log, looking at a booklet.

"Your mom brought this back from Oak Harbor," Thuy said. "Did you know that during the last ice age, all of Puget Sound was covered by a glacier a mile thick?"

"A mile?" Megan glanced up at the tall firs, trying to imagine that much ice above their heads.

"That's what it says here," Peter explained. "As the ice melted, the sea water rushed in to fill the Sound. The sand and gravel and boulders the glacier left behind cover the islands."

Thuy jumped to her feet. "Peter, here comes your father."

The three of them ran to meet him.

"No news yet," he said. "The marshal turned the case over to the Island County sheriff, who's passed the word to law enforcement officers all over the island."

Megan caught the worried look her mom gave Darren. Did they think something bad had happened to Dinh? "Isn't there something else we can do?" she cried.

"Thuy said her grandmother notified the police at home. We'll keep looking, of course," said Darren, "but I think the best thing for us is to go ahead and enjoy our holiday. We'll let the ranger know whenever we leave camp, in case someone tries to contact us."

Disappointment flashed across Thuy's face, but she nodded. "My brother is probably looking for me too," she said.

"I'm sure you're right," said Darren. He looked around at the group. "So how about exploring Ebey Prairie this morning?"

Everybody pitched in to pack a lunch and clean up the campsite. Megan was about to ask if she could drive when her stepfather slid behind the wheel of the minivan. Did he think she'd done a poor job of driving yesterday? But before she could ask, everyone else had piled in. She got in too.

Near Coupeville, Darren turned onto a road that crossed Ebey Prairie and headed toward the water glistening in the west. "What a view!" he exclaimed. "I'm surprised that developers haven't chopped this land into subdivisions."

"They'd like to," answered Sarah as Peter leaned out the window to wave at a farmer on a tractor. "But people here wanted to preserve their way of life and history. So they set up the first National Historical Reserve in the United States. This prairie, Ebey's Landing, and Coupeville are parts of it."

They slowed to watch workers harvesting potatoes. Thuy peered at them intently, but Dinh was not among them.

Megan studied her brochure. "There's an old pioneer cemetery near here. Isaac Ebey's buried there."

"With or without his head?" Peter asked.

Megan shuddered. "With it, I think. That must be the cemetery up there." She pointed north to where the fields sloped up to meet some woods.

"We can go there later, if you like," Darren said. "But first, let's check this out."

He made a sharp left turn into a dirt drive and stopped. Beyond a gate, the drive crossed a field to a weathered, two-story building standing empty and alone on the prairie. It leaned toward the sea. White curtains still hung in its windows.

"That's the old Ferry House," Sarah said. "Isaac Ebey's home was a few yards away. After his death the Ebey family built this inn to house island visitors."

"Can we go closer?" Peter asked his dad.

"I guess so, as long as you don't trample what's growing in the fields."

"Don't go into the building," cautioned Sarah. "It doesn't look safe."

"You're a worrywart, Mom." Megan grabbed her camera as she got out of the minivan. She squeezed after Peter between the bars of the gate. Thuy followed. The adults remained with the vehicle. Jiggs dashed ahead to snuffle among the vines and leaves where green globes of pumpkins were ripening to orange.

"Looks like a strong wind would blow the place

over," Peter commented as they neared it. "I wonder how long it's been there."

Megan snapped a picture, then studied her brochure. "Since 1860. Ebey's Landing is down there." She pointed to a ravine which broke the sharp edge where field met bluff. "It says here it was the best place to come ashore on the whole west side of the island."

They looked down on a curving gravel shore. "Can't you almost see the Indians pulling their dugouts up on that beach?" Thuy asked.

"Almost," agreed Megan. "The trail to the prairies and the Coupeville area came up this ravine. The Indians still used the trail, even after Ebey got a ferry service going that linked the landing to Seattle and Port Townsend."

"Did the ferry have something to do with him losing his head?" Peter questioned.

Megan laughed. "No. But—and pardon the pun—it *is* a hair-raising story."

They walked around the house but saw no sign of the original cabins of the Ebey homestead.

"Well?" asked Peter. "I'm waiting."

"Oh ... sorry," Megan said. "Even though island Indians were peaceful, there was fighting in other places. In 1855 and 1856, settlers worried about the fierce Haidas who raided from Canada. They built some blockhouses for protection, like the one we saw in Coupeville.

"When raiders made trouble at Port Gamble, across the Sound, a U.S. steamer fired on them and killed some of their chiefs or *tyees*. They decided to kill a white 'tyee' in revenge.

"One night warriors crept up the trail from the beach. When Isaac answered their knock, they shot him, cut off his head, and carried it away."

Peter grimaced. "That's gross!"

"Want to hear something even grosser?" Megan offered. "Some stories say his friend went to Canada and brought the head back. Some say he found just the scalp."

"Well," Peter said. "I guess Ebey learned the hard way it pays to keep your head when you're in trouble!" The girls groaned at the bad joke.

Thuy darted off. "Beat you back to the van."

Megan and Peter ran after her. A few minutes later they drove down a short, steep hill and stopped beside the beach at Ebey's Landing.

After reading a historical marker, the adults sat on driftwood to enjoy the sun, and Peter wandered with Thuy northward along the crescent-shaped beach. Jiggs galloped ahead of his master, startling gulls and sandpipers into the air. Scattered groups of people beachcombed or sat in the sun. Thuy, Megan knew, would be watching for a black-haired young man in a blue shirt. She decided to search in the other direction.

After being around so many people the past couple of days, she enjoyed the solitude. Soon the only sounds she could hear over the wind in her ears were the screams of the gulls and the crunch of water-rounded cobbles underfoot.

She stooped to turn a rock over. Baby crabs underneath scurried for shelter. They made her think of

Thuy. Those bullies on the wharf had turned her whole world upside down, like she'd just done to the little crabs. Even though Thuy tried to hide her worry, Megan knew she must be thinking about Dinh all the time.

She replaced the rock. "Please, Lord," she whispered. "Help us find Thuy's brother."

Not Just Fun and Games

Later, at the pioneers' cemetery on the hill, they scattered to wander among the headstones and monuments.

"So many headstones are for babies and children," Megan commented. "Or young people. Look. Here's a girl just my age who died of diphtheria."

Peter found a fenced-in plot containing a couple of tall monuments and several smaller ones. "Most of these last names are Ebey," he called.

Megan and Thuy ran to join him. "Here's Isaac's grave," Thuy said, reaching out to touch a moss and sand encrusted white stone shaft. They could decipher only part of the inscription. Megan turned to gaze across the prairie below. "There's the Ferry House and Ebey's Landing and all the lands that once belonged to him," she said. She posed Peter and Thuy beside the stone shaft and snapped their picture with the farmlands as background. Then they sauntered back to the minivan and sat down on the grass to wait for the adults. Jiggs trotted up and flopped beside them.

"Well," said Megan, "Two more days and we'll be back in school. I don't know whether to be happy or unhappy." At least she'd be near Sean, she thought. *If some other girl hadn't already snared him while she was off on this trip.*

"I thought I'd be glad," Thuy said in a small voice. "But how can I go back to school, or even home to Grandmother, without Dinh?"

"Don't worry, Thuy." Peter patted her hand. "We'll find him."

Megan hoped he was right. This sight-seeing was okay, but so far they'd made little progress in solving the mystery of Dinh's disappearance. Her mom and Darren were overdoing this family business. If only they didn't all have to do everything together, she could take Thuy and the minivan—Peter too, of course—and do more looking and asking questions. Somebody on this island must know where Dinh had gone.

Finally Sarah and Darren came back to the minivan. "You three look serious," Darren said.

"Thuy's worried about finding her brother," Megan said. "I am too. There must be something more we can do."

"We've notified the authorities," her mom said. "And you've put up posters and asked lots of questions. What else can we do?"

"I guess a cemetery isn't the best place in the world to look for him," Darren grinned. "How about driving into Coupeville for a cold drink?"

Megan shrugged. "Okay." They bought soft drinks at a small restaurant near the top of the hill. Leaving the minivan there, they took Sarah's suggestion to walk down toward the water. Restlessly, Megan waited while the others stopped to admire some of the Victorian-style houses and churches for which the town was known.

Signs told about some of the buildings. "Several of these houses once belonged to sea captains," Thuy commented.

"Penn Cove is such a protected harbor," Darren answered. "I suppose those old salts thought this was a good place to retire."

"I wouldn't mind living in such a picturesque little town someday." Megan's mom took her new husband's hand as they walked along. Darren smiled at his wife.

Peter, holding Jiggs' leash, walked ahead with Thuy. They laughed together over some joke Megan didn't hear. She felt left out and thought again of her missed opportunity to be with Sean and her other friends at the lake this weekend. She grimaced and turned away.

"Look!" Peter gasped and pointed toward the cross street ahead. "A brown van just went by!"

He and Jiggs dashed to the intersection with Thuy in hot pursuit. Megan ran after them. If there'd been a van, it was gone. "You're imagining things, Peter," Megan scoffed.

"It must have turned down Front Street. Come on!" Peter and Jiggs led the girls in a race to the next corner.

Megan rounded the corner and stopped. Half a block away, a shiny, dark brown vehicle pulled into a just-vacated parking space. "That van doesn't need paint or body work," she said with disgust. "What a wild goose chase!"

Peter wiped beads of sweat from his face. "It's a Ford and it's brown," he said defensively. "And I saw a dent in the back fender."

"I will talk to them," Thuy said. She took a deep breath and hurried to the van. She spoke to the driver. He shook his head. Thuy stepped back. "They just got here," she said, her shoulders slumping. "This is their first time on the island."

"Sorry," Peter muttered.

They walked back to the corner to meet the adults. "It was the wrong van," Thuy told them. They walked in silence back to their own vehicle.

Peter climbed in beside Jiggs and stared out the window as they drove toward Fort Ebey. Obviously he felt badly for causing Thuy another disappointment. I shouldn't have been so rough on him, Megan thought. Anybody can make a mistake. But she stubbornly kept her mouth closed.

"My, it's warm!" Sarah said when they reached their campsite. "I'm going to relax in the shade with my book. Okay if I cook dinner after it cools off a bit?"

"Fine," said her husband. "I'm going to stretch out in one of these lawn chairs and take a snooze."

The young people looked at each other. None of them felt ready to take it easy.

"Could we take the van and follow some of the back roads?" Megan asked her mother. "We could put up more posters and talk to people about Dinh."

Sarah exchanged glances with Darren. "Let's wait on that until one of us can go along."

"Don't you trust my driving?" Megan shot back.

"Your mother trusts your driving," Darren said in a tone that let her know she'd better be more respectful. "But if you had trouble, we wouldn't know where to look for you."

Peter glanced from his dad to Megan. "We could explore in the bunker," he suggested.

"We've already done that." Megan dismissed his suggestion. "I think I'll hike to the beach. Anyone else want to come?"

"It's too hot for hiking," protested Peter.

"It will be cooler by the water," Megan told him. "But if you can't walk that far, there's a beach we can drive to just north of here." She gave her stepfather a challenging look. "If nobody thinks I'll get lost."

Peter's face had reddened at her condescending tone. Thuy noticed and jumped to his defense. "I think it *is* too hot for hiking in the sun, especially after we've walked so much already today."

"Take the van," Darren said, impatience in his voice. "And see if you guys can't get along."

Already Darren and Peter were ganging up on her. Megan frowned and went to find her sketchbook and pencils. She climbed into the driver's seat, ignoring Peter, Thuy, and Jiggs in the backseat. They drove along a tree-shaded road in silence. She parked beside a log railing. A few picnic tables were scattered among the trees, and in front of them a trail led down a ravine toward the beach.

"Lock your doors," she commanded, putting the key in her pocket and locking the driver's side door. Sketchbook in hand, she stalked away down the trail without waiting for the others. Jiggs crashed past and ran ahead of her.

At the edge of the woods, Megan stopped. "Oh, look at all the driftwood!" she whispered. Winter storms had tossed hundreds of big logs over a ridge of dunes, fitting them together against the base of the curving bluff like puzzle pieces arranged by some giant's hand.

Her sour mood evaporated as she played follow-the-leader with Jiggs on the driftwood. Then she wandered down the sloping beach, checking to see what shells the waves had brought in.

Just as she began to wonder where Peter and Thuy were, they burst over the ridge of dunes, laughing. They hesitated when they saw Megan and looked at each other.

"Find anything?" Peter called. Megan held up a moon snail shell.

Peter and Thuy looked at each other again and giggled. What was so funny, anyway? "I'm going to wade," Thuy told Peter. Thuy dropped her shoes and socks on a flat rock and ran to splash along the edge of the waves. Peter took off his sneakers too and tested the water with a bare foot.

"Brrr! This will cool us off. Come on," he yelled to Megan.

"No thanks." Megan watched the two laughing and splashing. Jiggs romped with them and barked. She retreated to the shade of a driftwood log and began to sketch the curving shoreline, the bluff, and the others playing.

After a while, Thuy came and sat down to watch her draw. Peter and Jiggs joined them. Suddenly Thuy hopped up and ran to look at something caught under a piece of driftwood. She pulled out a faded blue rag, looked at it, then dropped it. Slowly she walked back to the others.

"It's blue, like Dinh's shirt," she said. "But it's just an old towel."

Megan saw the sympathy on Peter's face. He stood up. "Hey, Thuy, I'll race you to the bluff down there," he said. Thuy's woebegone expression vanished. She was off in a flash. Sand spurted over Megan's sketchbook as Peter churned after her.

Jiggs got up and started after them but didn't follow. "What's the matter, Jiggs? Did they wear you out?" She shook the sand off the sketchbook and closed it. Absently she sorted through some multicolored pebbles washed up against the base of her log. Despite his nonsense, Peter was pretty understanding for a boy, she thought. If she had to have a stepbrother, she could have done worse. She picked out a couple of translucent green stones and held them to the light.

They were just bits of water-worn glass. But she put them in her pocket and wandered along the beach, pondering. The ocean could grind and polish something as useless as broken glass and make it beautiful. There must be a lesson there. Something about God using hard things to smooth out rough edges in people's lives? Coming to the beach had been a good idea. She felt more peaceful than she had all afternoon.

Peter and Thuy came panting back.

"Time to go, you guys," she told them. She left Peter and Thuy putting on their socks and shoes and followed the trail back to the parking lot. She unlocked the van's doors, climbed into the driver's seat, and inserted the key in the ignition. As Jiggs and the other two came into sight in the ravine, she turned the key. The starter ground, but the engine didn't turn over.

Now what? She got out and raised the hood of the

vehicle. Baffled, she peered into its innards.

Peter came up. "What's wrong, Megan?" he asked.

"The van won't start, that's what's wrong."

"Is it out of gas?" Thuy asked.

"Maybe it's something with the starter," suggested Peter.

She glanced at them, exasperated. "It's got gas, and the starter works. It's something else." She bent over and jiggled some important looking wires.

"Want me to look?" Peter asked.

Megan scowled. "What could you do that I can't do?" She wiggled a couple of hoses and got back behind the steering wheel. Again she ground the starter.

"Better let me look, Megan. I'm used to helping my dad work on our truck, remember?" Peter said with barely concealed glee.

Suspicious, she got out and slammed the door. She glared at him and at Thuy, whose grin had turned into a half-worried, half-guilty expression. She stalked away to get a drink at the campground spigot.

Peter did something under the hood. He walked around to the other side of the engine and checked the battery terminals. "I don't see anything wrong, Megan," he called. "Maybe we'd better start walking."

"Go ahead if you want to. I'm going to stay with the van." Megan climbed in and turned the key. This time the engine caught.

Peter's face turned red with suppressed laughter.

"I thought so. You did something to it, didn't you?" she said to him.

"What did I do?" Peter asked.

"Never mind. Get in." Thuy looked even guiltier. "That wasn't funny," Megan said angrily. "What if I tell your dad you fooled around with the van, Peter?"

"Do you really want to do that?" asked Peter. "Remember what he said about getting along?"

"I didn't do anything to you ..." Megan scowled at her stepbrother. "You just don't like it because I can drive and you can't."

"It's not that," Peter said. "I'm glad you can drive us places. But that doesn't give you the right to be bossy. Or insulting."

"Peter," Thuy said, "we shouldn't have played such a mean trick. I'm sorry, Megan, really I am. We just thought it would be funny ..."

"All I did was take the rotor out," Peter said to Megan. "It didn't hurt anything. Don't be mad."

Megan sat a moment without speaking. "I guess I was pretty obnoxious," she said to them.

"Thuy's right. It was a bad idea," Peter answered. "We've got to work as a team if we're going to find Dinh."

Megan nodded. "We didn't ask to be a team, but we do have to act like one. Peter, I haven't been very nice to you sometimes. And it's not your fault. I'm sorry."

Peter's face crumpled a little. "Forget it. It's easier for me than for you. I know my mom can't come back, ever." His voice thickened and trailed off. "Even if she wanted to." He punched Megan's arm lightly. "I've always wanted a sister, so you're stuck with me. Come on, driver, let's get back before they come looking for us."

"It's been a long day," Megan said, sitting down on a piece of firewood next to her mother. She stretched and yawned. At the campfire Peter and Thuy toasted marshmallows on straightened wire coat hangers.

"It's been a fun day," said Thuy. "Except I wish we had found Dinh."

"We'll keep praying," Darren Lewis said. "When we can't help ourselves, we can depend on God to help us."

"Do you think God knows where my brother is?"

"Of course He does. Where's the Bible, Megan?"

Megan found it and brought it to Darren. He leafed through the pages until he found the spot he was looking for. Marking the place with his finger, he handed the book to Thuy.

"Read what Jesus said here."

Thuy read aloud the verses he pointed to. "Are not five sparrows sold for two pennies? Yet not one of them is forgotten by God. Indeed, the very hairs of your head are all numbered. Don't be afraid; you are worth more than many sparrows." Thuy looked up. "Oh, I hope that means He's watching over Dinh!" she said.

"It does," Sarah told Thuy. "God loves Dinh and you very much. He is watching over both of you."

"Where are we going to church tomorrow?" Peter asked.

"We saw some nice old churches in Coupeville," his stepmother replied. "Would you like to visit one of them?"

"That would be fun," said Peter. "Thuy, what church do you go to?"

"My grandmother is Buddhist," Thuy answered. "But before I was born, my parents went to the Catholic church in Vietnam. Sometimes Dinh and I go to the one in Madrona Bay."

"I haven't seen a Catholic church. But that pretty little church on the street entering Coupeville is Lutheran," Megan said. "The one with the sign that says, 'House of the Lord.'"

"House of the Lord," said Darren Lewis. "I like that. Shall we go there tomorrow?"

Megan knew Darren was trying to make Thuy feel comfortable. She smiled and looked up. Stars twinkled through the branches above their heads.

Her mother began to sing a song about not being discouraged or sad because God's "eye is on the sparrow, and I know He watches me."

Megan listened, humming along. Thuy slipped away to the tent and came back with her flute. She picked up the melody and played softly.

The song ended. "Play some more, Thuy," Peter urged. She began a piece with complicated trills and runs. At first Megan didn't recognize the music. Then she realized that Thuy had taken the simple melody they'd just sung and turned it into a piece fit for a concert hall.

Other campers gathered to listen outside their campfire circle. Thuy's face glowed as she effortlessly moved into another piece. The notes sang out through the hushed forest.

The campfire, stars, four people becoming a new family ... and Thuy Nguyen and her flute. Sean Bertram could wait. And somehow, tonight Megan saw the thoughts of her own father for what they really were ... fantasies and daydreams. She knew she would never forget this night.

The Brown Van Again

Water droplets beaded every twig and leaf when Megan and Thuy crawled out of their tent next morning. Fog lay like a damp gray blanket over their camp and muffled the waking-up noises from other campsites.

"Good morning!" Darren Lewis stood sleepy-eyed over the fireplace, crumpling newspaper and arranging a tepee of kindling over it. "Did you girls rest well?"

"Fine, thank you," Thuy answered.

Megan hugged herself and bounced in place to stop her shivering. "I slept okay, but I got cold."

Peter, auburn hair sticking up in all directions, appeared out of the fog. He dropped an armload of firewood by the fireplace. "Lucky we saw the ranger going by with that truckload of wood, Dad." He held his hands over the flames crackling through the kindling. "I hope this fog goes away in time for us to go fishing after church."

"It will," Darren predicted. He fed some of the smaller sticks of firewood to the blaze. "It's just a change-of-season fog. The sun will soon burn it off."

"Tomorrow is Labor Day. But it doesn't seem like it should be fall already," Megan said. "One day left before school, not counting today."

"You three will have plenty to tell about when you

have to write that 'What-I-Did-this-Summer' essay," Darren said.

"Yes," Thuy said. "Oh, I hope we'll find Dinh today."

The forlorn note in Thuy's voice prompted Megan to give her slender shoulders a squeeze. "Don't get discouraged," she told her. "Come on, let's roll up our sleeping bags and see what we can find to wear to church."

A few minutes later the girls joined Peter as he took Jiggs for a run on the meadow below the gun emplacements. The edge of the grassland disappeared into gray nothingness. A fog horn moaned, and invisible sea gulls cried. "It's so lonesome out here," Thuy said. "I'm glad I'm not still hiding in the brush."

"Me too," Peter said. Jiggs came back from his explorations, and they all raced back to the warmth of the campfire and breakfast.

"Mom," Megan said as they ate, "I hope you realize that all we have to wear to church are our camping clothes."

"I'm sure the people there are used to visitors coming as they are," Sarah answered. "Besides, we won't have to come back here to change."

In Coupeville, the sun was burning through the fog as they parked the minivan and the boat on its trailer. Peter rolled down the windows for Jiggs and told him to guard the van.

Thuy climbed out and hitched her ever-present knapsack to her shoulders. "Do you think we can say a prayer for Dinh this morning?" she whispered to Megan.

"Of course we can," Megan said, although she wasn't sure what to expect in a church that was different from her own. "I asked God to be with Dinh before I got up. God listens to our prayers no matter where we are."

The bell in the steeple rang as they walked to the little frame church. Women and girls with sweaters over their summer dresses, men in suits and ties, other campers, and bicyclists in stretch shorts all streamed up the steps and through the double doors.

"Where are you folks from?" a friendly usher asked them at the door.

"Madrona Bay," Peter answered.

"Welcome." The usher turned to greet Megan and the others.

"Excuse me, sir," Peter said. The usher turned back to him. Quickly Peter told him about Dinh. "Do you think ..." He hesitated.

The usher finished his sentence. "We could ask the congregation if anyone has seen him? I don't know why not. I'll talk to Pastor John."

The usher seated them and slipped through a side door. Megan looked around at the mulberry-colored upholstered pews and carpet. The glass in the tall windows was stained mostly mulberry and teal blue. Some things looked different from their church at home, but the cross behind the altar was familiar—so was the board that announced the hymn numbers. An organist played soft music.

The usher came back through the side door, followed by the pastor in his vestments. The pastor bowed before the altar, then greeted the congregation. Megan and Peter watched the other worshipers and stood when they stood, knelt when they knelt. When the pastor began to talk about loving one's neighbor, Megan felt at home. Their own minister might have said the same things.

At the end of the service, the pastor made announcements. Then he said, "We have a young visitor today who has had a sad experience in our town. Thuy Nguyen, would you come up here?"

Thuy looked flustered, but she walked to the front and stood beside the pastor. He briefly told the congregation what had happened to her and Dinh. "Could you tell us what your brother looks like, Thuy?"

Shyly, Thuy looked up at the pastor. "He's shorter than you, and much thinner."

A ripple of laughter went through the crowd and Thuy's golden cheeks turned rosy. "He has black hair and a nice smile. He's almost 18 years old."

"Thank you, Thuy. Dinh was last seen climbing into an old brown van, possibly a Ford, which needed body work and paint," the pastor told the congregation. "If you know anything that will help this young lady in her search, please tell her or phone the Coupeville police."

After the service, the family shook hands with the pastor. As they walked down the steps, many of the congregation members greeted them. Several of the hikers and bicyclists promised to watch for Dinh.

As the crowd thinned, Megan said to Thuy, "Aren't you glad we came here this morning? There'll be more people looking for your brother now."

"Yes, I am glad," Thuy answered. "I hope someone will see him soon."

"Young lady! Young lady!" An elderly woman with a

cane stood at the top of the steps. The usher they'd talked to earlier helped her make her way down and over to them. Lively black eyes twinkled in her lined face. "I was afraid you'd leave before I could catch you. Did you say the van your brother got into was old and dented?"

"Yes, and it needed painting."

"I'm visiting from Langley today," said the woman. "This may be of no help to you at all, but I've seen a van like that in Langley many times. I believe it is a Ford."

"Maybe it's the one!" Thuy exclaimed. "Do you know who owns it?"

"I'm sorry. I don't."

"But it's a clue! Thank you!" Thuy shook the lady's hand.

~~~~~~~~~~~~~~~~~~

A short time later, they all sat in the sunshine at an outdoor lunch stand. Over hot dogs and milkshakes, they discussed what the woman had told Thuy.

"If Dinh is somewhere else on the island, the city marshal may want to get the sheriff in on this too," said Darren Lewis.

"But that would take a long time," Peter said. "How far is Langley?"

"It's down-island, about a 40-minute drive, I'd guess," his father answered. "We bypassed it our first day here when we drove up-island from the ferry."

"Could we go there and try to find who owns the van ourselves?" Thuy asked. She glanced hopefully at Peter. Then she said, "No. You planned to go fishing today. I don't want to spoil that."

"I don't care that much for fishing," Megan said. "I could drive Thuy to Langley and help her look."

"I can fish another time," Peter said. "May all three of us go?"

Darren looked at their eager faces. "What do you think?" he asked his wife.

"How would you set about finding the van's owner?" Sarah wanted to know.

"Well," Megan said, "we'll ask people ... in the shops and businesses, and put up our posters."

"We could talk to the Langley police," Peter said.

"I guess it wouldn't hurt for the kids to see what they can find out," Sarah told Darren. "If they promise to be careful."

"All right then," Darren said, his blue eyes crinkling behind his glasses. "Take the van. We don't mind fishing by ourselves." He pulled out his billfold and turned to Megan. "The van's got gas, but here's some extra money for snacks or emergencies." He handed her a twenty. "Look to see if the boat is docked at the wharf when you get back. If we're not there, wait for us at the public launch ramp."

Darren could have given Peter the money, but he'd given it to her, the oldest, just as a father would in a real family. Megan smiled. "Thanks," she said.

"That's a long drive for them," Sarah said to Darren, sounding a little worried. "If they're delayed or have trouble, we need to set up a way to communicate."

"We could leave messages at the restaurant on the wharf," suggested Peter.

"Fine," said his dad.

Darren and Sarah walked with the young people to the floats at the end of the wharf to be sure the Good Fortune was all right. Then they checked at the restaurant to see if they could leave telephone messages. Peter wrote the restaurant's phone number on a scrap of paper and put it in his pocket.

They drove out of town to the launch ramp. They put the boat into the water, then parked and unhitched the trailer. Megan got behind the minivan's steering wheel. Peter, Thuy, and Jiggs climbed in.

"Drive carefully," called Darren and Sarah as they pulled away. "God go with you!"

"Thanks," Megan called out the window. "See you later." They were off to search for Dinh. Maybe this would be the day they'd solve the mystery of his disappearance!

~~~~~~~~~~~~~~~~~~~~~~~~

South of Coupeville, the drier, more open country gave way to thick forests. "We've just passed out of ... some kind of shadow of the Olympics," Megan remarked.

"Some kind of what?" asked Peter.

"The rain shadow, I think," she said. "When wet ocean air hits the Olympic mountains it rises, cools, and drops the moisture on the west side of the Olympics. So it's dry when it crosses north Whidbey. The air moving over south Whidbey has bypassed the Olympics, so it still has its moisture. You can tell it rains more here. There are more trees."

"If you say so."

"It's true! It's so dry near Fort Ebey that in some places you can even find cactus growing."

After what seemed a long while, they turned off the main north-south highway and followed a narrower, winding road through the woods to Langley. The village spilled down the slope in front of them and along a bluff overlooking Saratoga Passage.

People milled everywhere as Megan inched the minivan into town. Looking down the first cross street at the bottom of the hill, she saw that the main street along the bluff was barricaded against traffic. "It's some kind of a street fair," she said.

"If Dinh is here, how will we ever find him among all these people?" Thuy worried.

"There are cars everywhere," Peter complained. "We'll never find a place to park."

"Lighten up, you guys. And keep your eyes open for a brown van," Megan said.

The slow-moving stream of traffic passed the fire station and the post office. Megan hit the brakes as a car pulled out of a space just ahead. "Thanks, Lord." She eased into the vacated spot and cut the engine. "We're here. Where do we start?"

"Maybe we should give the place a once over first," Peter suggested. "Find out where the police station is, look for places to post our fliers ..."

"Oh, the fliers." Megan picked up the remaining posters and handed them to Thuy to put in her knapsack. She looped her camera strap around her neck.

Peter snapped the leash to Jiggs's collar as they got out and locked the doors. The town library occupied a wedge of land across the street. The main road leading into town bordered the other side of the wedge. They crossed both streets to a path bordering a steep embankment and gazed down on a marina crowded with boats. "Would Dinh look for work at a place like that?" Peter asked Thuy.

"He might," she answered. "How do we get down?"

"This way." Peter led them down a steep drive to the water's edge. They scanned the boats but saw few people.

"Everyone must be at the street fair," Megan said. "Let's see if we can leave a poster here at least."

As they came out of the marina office, they heard raucous laughter. Two men reeled toward them down the steep drive, each with a garishly made-up woman on his arm. The women wore dark glasses and skimpy shorts. Their arms were loaded with stuffed toys and other souvenirs of the street fair; each of the men carried six-packs of beer.

"Oh, no!" gasped Thuy, shrinking against Peter. "Those men!"

"What's the matter?" Megan asked. Thuy trembled. Megan took a closer look at the men. One of them was squat with powerful shoulders and a large head thrust forward on a short, thick neck. The other man was taller with a slouching walk and a self-satisfied smirk on his hatchet face.

"Oh, Buffalo," squealed the woman with the first man. "You're so funny!"

"Those men ..." Thuy whispered faintly. "They're the ones who hurt Dinh!"

Megan stepped in front of the other two, casually

turning her back to the four people coming down the drive. "Act like you're paying no attention to them," she said in a low voice. "Thuy, you're positive?"

"Yes," she said. "I remember now. I even heard one man call the other 'Buffalo.'"

Megan steered the others to a spot across the parking lot where they could keep an eye on the four adults making their unsteady way down the ramp to the floats. "We can't stop them by ourselves," she said. "Watch what they do. I'll go to the marina's office and call the Langley police."

The two couples attempted to board a boat tied at the far end of the dock. "Is that the same boat, Thuy?" she asked.

"I don't know. I never saw their boat."

Thinking quickly, Megan said, "They might recognize you, Thuy, but they'd never suspect me or Peter. You take Jiggs and go call the police. Peter, come on." She checked to see if there was film left in her camera. "You and I will be tourists."

Megan started toward the dock. Peter followed.

"For crying out loud, Megan. What are we going to do?" Peter asked.

"Pretend to be interested in the boats. If we can get a description of their boat, that would help the police. Especially if we don't find Dinh soon."

"Oh, okay." Peter followed her down the grated metal ramp to the dock. "Megan, what if we don't find him? I didn't want to say this in front of Thuy, but what if he's not on the island? Maybe we'll never find him."

"That's why we need to get all the evidence we can

against those men," she answered. Trying to appear casual, the two strolled past the boats.

"There's one from British Columbia," Peter exclaimed, pretending great interest.

Megan aimed her camera at the flags fluttering from its mast.

Aboard the white pleasure craft near the end of the dock, the two women shrieked with laughter as Buffalo hugged them both at once. They disappeared into the cabin with their purchases.

Buffalo began to fiddle with the inboard motor. "What's the matter, Ole, too many thumbs?" he called to the hatchet-faced man on the dock trying to unfasten the lines holding the boat.

"Its name is the *Sister Susie*," Peter whispered. "The same boat that almost hit the ferry!" Megan saw his lips move as he repeated the numbers painted on the end of the boat.

She framed the stern in her viewfinder and snapped a picture just as Buffalo looked up from the motor and saw her. Good, she thought. That should show Buffalo's face clearly.

"Nice boat you've got there, mister," Peter said. Megan knew he was hoping to delay them until the police got there. "How's the fishing today?"

Buffalo jerked his head toward the women in the cabin and winked at his friend on the dock. He roared with laughter at his own cleverness. "Great. Just great."

Megan hid her discomfort as Ole moved closer, leering at her. She spoke to Buffalo. "I've heard salmon fishing isn't as good as it used to be, with all the immigrants moving in and catching fish too," Megan said, trying to keep her expression innocent. "Is that true?"

Ole stumbled over the cleat holding the rope he was trying to cast off. His hatchet face turned a darker red. He answered for himself and Buffalo. "Yeah, it's true. Should chase all them Chinks off the water."

The man bent closer to her. "Wanna know what I do every time I get a chance?"

Megan recoiled from the blast of his boozy breath. "Wha ... what do you do?"

She never found out. Just then Buffalo got the motor started. Over its noise he yelled at Ole to throw him the line and get aboard. She snapped one last picture as the high-powered boat roared away, just missing a couple of others at anchor in the harbor.

"Good going, Megan!" Peter grinned. "But you took a big chance, asking that question about immigrants."

"Maybe. But we found out how they feel, didn't we?"

"Sure did." Peter walked beside her along the float. "I'd like to see someone get those guys off the water. What's a 'chink,' anyhow?"

"It's an old slang term, not very nice, for a Chinese person. He's lumping all Asians together."

They saw Thuy and Jiggs coming toward them. "Sorry, Thuy," she called. "We tried to keep them talking until the police got here. I did get some good pictures of the men and the boat."

"I'm glad you did," said Thuy. "The police aren't coming. The dispatcher said they're all busy with the street fair. Since no crime was being committed, she couldn't send anybody."

"Isn't beating up somebody a crime?" Peter cried.

"That's what I said. But she said it didn't happen here. We'll have to talk to the sheriff in Coupeville, I guess."

"Then let's talk to him," he said. "Where's the pay phone, Thuy?"

She took them inside the marina store. They looked up the number for the Coupeville sheriff's department. Peter dialed, listened a moment, then hung up. "Answering machine," he said. "We'll have to try again later."

Jiggs tugged and frisked as the three of them plodded up the drive to the bluff. They joined the crowds of people moving along First Street toward the picturesque old buildings of the business district. As at Coupeville, the businesses on one side of the street perched on the bluff's edge. In a space between buildings, a bronze statue of a boy and another of his dog gazed out over Saratoga passage.

"Hey, you two, let me take your picture," Megan said. Thuy and Peter struck poses beside the statues. Megan snapped the shutter just as Jiggs stretched his neck to sniff the strange dog lying beside his bronze master.

People swarmed past booths of colorful wares, looking and buying. After the experience they'd just had, Megan felt a little disoriented by the festive atmosphere. She sat down on a bench near the statues. She watched a man nearby cutting out wooden toys and garden ornaments; another booth featured local watercolor prints; one sold leather goods; and another displayed quilts and needlework.

Children wandered by with cotton candy; whiffs of spicy cookery teased her nostrils. Two young men strummed guitars. Over all the sounds came the tinkle of an ice-cream cart.

"Where should we start?" Megan asked the others.

"Don't start yet. I'll get us some ice-cream bars," Peter said. He dodged around a group of people and signaled the cart's driver to stop. The ice-cream man waited while Peter chose what he wanted, then scooted away to his next customers.

Peter handed them each a toffee bar. The smooth ice cream and crunchy chocolate coating melted in Megan's mouth. Jiggs crowded close to the bench and nudged her, drooling. "You can have my last bite," she promised.

Peter finished his ice cream. "We can't ask all these hundreds of people if they've seen Dinh," he said. "We can't take Jiggs into the stores either."

"What if two of us ask in the businesses and leave posters there?" offered Thuy. "The third person could check at the booths."

"I don't mind keeping Jiggs and doing the booths," Megan said. "Why don't you take one side of the street, Thuy? Peter can take the other. When you meet, you can help me. Or I can help you if I finish first."

"You'll probably finish first," Peter said. "Don't forget, we passed businesses where we first came into town, and there's the cross street too."

Megan held out the last of her ice cream for Jiggs to slurp from the stick. Then she took his leash and walked to the first booth. Peter and Thuy disappeared into the stores.

Over and over Megan told the story of Thuy's missing brother. Sometimes she had to wait while the proprietor of the booth talked to a customer. Then she scanned the faces of the people passing by. If only Thuy had a picture of Dinh.

One booth had a big banner reading "Save the Planet for Our Children." On the walls, posters and pamphlets advertised conservation organizations. The young man inside did not seem very busy so Megan spent longer than usual telling him the story.

"You say your friend is a fisherman?" The man's eyes glinted behind thick glasses. "Have you seen this brochure on what overfishing is doing to our oceans?"

"No, I haven't." Megan took the brochure. "I just want to know if you might have seen a young Vietnamese man in town recently."

The man shook his head. Then he looked past Megan's shoulder, and a pleased smile spread across his face.

"Talk about coincidence! I'll bet that's your friend, right there!"

══The "Save the Planet" Farm

Megan whirled and looked into a pair of slant-ed black eyes in a round, cheerful face. The man had short, straight black hair. Around his neck he carried an expensive camera.

He nodded politely and melted back into a group of tourists. Tourists from Japan!

"Thanks anyway," Megan told the booth's proprietor.

She steered Jiggs around a crowd of little kids watching a clown make balloon animals and went on to the next booth, which sold floppy cinnamon-sprinkled pastries called elephant ears. A woman gave one to her little boy in his stroller and paid for the treat. Megan stepped up to the counter, then turned when she heard the woman laugh.

Jiggs sat obediently beside her, taking dainty bites from the elephant ear the little boy held out for him.

"Oh, Jiggs," Megan exclaimed, pulling him away. "I'm sorry," she said to the mother. "I'll buy your son a new one."

"Don't worry about it. Brandon wouldn't eat it all any-way." She tore off the piece her little boy had been holding and gave it back to him. The rest she tossed to Jiggs.

Old-time fiddle music sounded from up the street. Megan worked her way from booth to booth, finally reaching the makeshift bandstand where the fiddlers played. People swayed to the music or sat on the pavement, listening, or wandered past to Anthes Avenue, the cross street where she had first noticed the fair.

Megan's legs suddenly felt very tired. Edging her way through the crowd toward the musicians, she sat down on the curb. Jiggs plopped beside her. She glanced at a group of tourists nearby, but she saw no one who might be Dinh.

"Sitting down on the job! Caught you!" Peter's voice came from close at hand. Megan jumped and Peter laughed. "Any luck?"

"Not really," she said, hoisting herself to her feet. The band struck up a loud and lively tune, and they backed away from the amplifiers. "Where's Thuy?" Megan asked.

"Here I am." Thuy squirmed through the crowd. "I didn't find anyone who's seen Dinh. A few people said they'd seen a van like we're looking for, but no one knew who owns it."

Peter looked at his watch. "It's after four. We don't have much time left."

"We'd better stop at the police station," Megan said.

"I was just there." Peter turned and pointed. "It's a few doors down this street—Anthes Avenue. The clerk said they'd received a bulletin from Coupeville. But she didn't remember a van that fits the description. She said one of the officers might if we came back later." He paused. "She did take my description of the Sister Susie and its operators."

The three edged out of the crowd around the bandstand and walked along the avenue. The city hall building, which housed the police department, sat just past an alley leading behind the First Street business establishments.

Peter stuck his head through an open door and spoke to someone inside. "The officers aren't back yet," he told the others.

"Let's see what's down this alley," Thuy suggested.

Parked vehicles crowded the spaces behind the shops. People milled in and out of back doors or took shortcuts between First and Second streets.

"Excuse me." A tall, slim man in bib overalls and no shirt brushed by with a wooden box of carrots in his muscular arms. He carried it through the back entrance of a store.

"That store's an interesting place," Peter said. "I talked to the people in there. They have groceries and clothes and tools and all kinds of other things."

"Like an old-fashioned general store?" asked Megan. When Peter nodded yes, she suggested, "Let's take a minute to look."

They squeezed close to the wall of the building to let a pickup camper back out of its parking space into the alley. The man in bib overalls brushed by again, arms empty, and Peter and Thuy started through an open hall toward the back entrance. Megan, still holding the leash, looked for a place to tie Jiggs.

Wondering what else the man might bring in, she watched him go to his vehicle, which had been hidden by the pickup camper. The man slammed the double back doors of his van, hopped in the front seat, and started the engine. The battered old van swung across the alley and down a short lane which connected to Second Street.

The battered old *brown* van! Megan practically choked in her haste to get words out. "Thuy! Peter! Come back. Hurry ... it's the van!"

They heard her shout and scrambled back outside. Peter saw the vehicle pulling into the street. He ran after it, yelling "Wait!" but the driver didn't hear. He turned right. By the time the others caught up with Peter the vehicle was a block and a half away, accelerating up the hill.

"It was the van," Peter panted. "I'm sure it was the van this time!"

"It had to be the one," Megan said. "Did anybody get the license number?" They stared at each other. Peter slapped his forehead in disgust.

"I think it had two zeroes in it," said Thuy.

"That's all right. The store manager probably knows who owns it," Megan said.

Peter took Jiggs' leash from Megan, and they hurried back to the grocery store. After Peter tied Jiggs to a railing, they went inside to a checkout counter.

"Could we speak to your produce manager?" Megan asked the young clerk.

"He's probably in the back room." The girl pointed to a pair of swinging doors they'd passed on the way in.

In a cool storeroom, they found a middle-aged man wearing a canvas apron over his ample stomach, tying carrots into bunches.

"Sir, who was the man who brought you those carrots?" Peter asked.

The man looked over the top of his glasses at him. "Why do you ask?"

"We're trying to help our friend here find her brother. He was last seen in Coupeville, getting into a brown van like the one that man drove away from your store."

"There are lots of brown vans," the man said.

"We know," Megan said, trying to keep her voice calm. "But that one fits the description we have. We think Dinh may have been hurt. Perhaps the driver was trying to help him."

"Please, sir," Thuy begged. "I've got to find my brother!"

The manager's face softened as he looked at Thuy. "Oh, all right. His name is Rex Hopner. He brings me organically grown produce from what the locals call the 'Save-the-Planet Farm.' "

Megan remembered the booth with the big "Save the Planet for the Children" banner. "Why do you call it that?"

"Oh, they're big on ecology, conservation, all that stuff. They have some funny ideas mixed in with it. Nice enough people, though," he added. "There's a whole group of them."

"Can you tell us how to get there?" Peter asked.

"Why don't you just telephone?"

Megan glanced at Thuy and answered the man in a low voice. "I think Dinh would have called his grandmother if everything was all right. Perhaps he didn't tell Rex, or whoever picked him up, who he was. Maybe they just gave him a ride somewhere. It would be better to talk to them in person."

Thuy heard Megan's words. Her eyes widened in dismay. "I didn't think of that," she said. "Maybe the driver can't help us. Even if Dinh is working for money to take us home, he would have called Grandmother."

"Let's not worry about the maybes until we talk to the people at the farm," Peter said to her.

The produce manager tore a paper towel from a roll on the counter. With his black marking pen he drew a map and handed it to Megan. "Go north out of town. Turn here, then here. After that it's not so plainly marked. There'll be several little roads heading off to the right. It's the second, maybe the third. I've never been in there myself. But I remember seeing a sign."

They thanked the man, retrieved Jiggs, and hurried to where they'd parked the minivan.

"We must have gone right past the road to the farm on our way into Langley," Megan said as she drove back up the hill.

After several miles, Thuy called, "There's the first turn."

They wound through the woods for what seemed like a long way, then turned again onto a road more twisty and narrow than the first.

"There's a drive to the right," Peter said. "That can't be it. It's too grassy to be used much."

"The produce man said it was the second or third driveway," reminded Thuy.

Megan drove in watchful silence. "Here's the second drive, but there's no sign."

"Keep going," Peter directed.

Just as the main road turned sharply, they came to a third drive. A sign above a mailbox read "Greentree Farm."

Peter and Thuy slid closer to the windshield. They peered ahead as Megan turned at the mailbox and crept along the rutted lane. Clinging white-knuckled to the steering wheel, she dodged to miss big trees and wound around and between small hills.

As they drove past tall trees and clumps of giant sword fern dotting the jumbled terrain, Thuy seemed to be concentrating only on the track ahead. A week ago today Dinh had disappeared, Megan thought. Who knows if we'll find him? No wonder she's tense.

They went deeper and deeper into the woods. "I wonder if the man at the store gave us the wrong directions," Peter said, craning to look up at the towering evergreens. "The sign said 'Greentree Farm.' I'll bet this is a tree farm."

"I hope we don't get stuck back here," Megan said.

Just then they jounced around a hill. A gate blocked the road, and several cars were parked near it. Megan pulled in next to one of the cars. She released a huge sigh of relief and switched off the ignition. Through the trees, they saw buildings and open spaces and the glimmer of a small lake.

"Good driving, Megan," Peter said.

"Thanks." She shrugged but was nevertheless pleased. "I don't see the brown van, do you?"

"Could it be in a garage?" Thuy ventured.

"Or maybe the driver had other errands and isn't back yet," Peter said. "Stay, Jiggs." Peter opened the windows so he could leave Jiggs in the minivan and got out. "Want your knapsack, Thuy?"

Thuy took it from him. "Thanks."

They crossed a wooden bridge over a stream and neared some women working in a garden. "Oh, it's beautiful here," Thuy murmured. "Look." She pointed to a deer nibbling grass beside the stream. At the sound of her voice, the animal raised its head and gazed at them, then like a shadow, vanished into the underbrush.

They walked on toward the garden. Beds of flowers and vegetables and herbs reminded Megan of an old-fashioned crazy quilt. A couple of women glanced up from their weeding; a third woman, who looked familiar, came toward them as they descended some steps from the driveway. They heard her humming to herself.

Removing her garden gloves, she pushed her long hair away from her face. "Hello! What can we do for you?"

"We're looking for Greentree Farm," Peter spoke up. "At least, I think we are. The man in town called it the 'Save the Planet Farm.'"

The woman smiled. "Some people call us that. You're at the right place."

"You have a very nice garden," Thuy said politely.

"This is only one of our gardens. Did you want to see someone in particular?"

"We'd like to see Rex Hopner," Megan answered.

"Rex? He drove in not too long ago. I'll ask if anyone knows where he is. Want to come along? You can see some of the farm while we look for him."

"That would be great," Megan answered for all of them.

"I'm Tonya." They introduced themselves, then followed Tonya past the biggest Madrona tree Megan had ever seen. The bare red trunk of this one must have rooted here a hundred years ago or more, she thought. A tire swing hung from one of the massive branches, sheltered from the sun by shiny evergreen leaves.

"Do you sometimes work in a bookstore in Coupeville?" she asked their guide.

"Why yes. I help here on my days off," Tonya answered. "I thought I'd seen you girls before. Didn't you buy some music a day or two ago?"

"I did," Thuy said. "Some Mozart, for my flute."

They reached a sprawling shingled building where stained-glass sun catchers brightened the windows. Strings of exotic bells hung on the porch.

"This is our headquarters and conference center," Tonya explained. "We're getting ready for a meeting next week." She led them through a big room to a kitchen with restaurant-type ranges. A huge kettle of soup simmered on one of them. A woman sat at a counter grinding grain in a noisy electric mill. She turned it off when she saw them.

"Hi, Louann," Tonya said. "Have you seen Rex?"

The woman smiled and shook her head.

"Louann plans to bake bread tomorrow," Tonya told them. She led them out the back door to a terraced patio with a lily pond. A man sat next to the pond, cross-legged, eyes closed, perfectly still. A faint shadow marked where hair used to grow on his shaven head.

"Is he all right?" Peter asked.

"Oh yes," Tonya answered. "He's just meditating ... getting in touch with the cosmic consciousness."

She led them along a path between storage buildings, onto a sloping lawn. A young man in overalls ambled from a cottage half-hidden in the woods above. A tousle-headed little boy rode on his shoulders.

"Terrel and his wife are the caretakers here," Tonya said. "His son is Jason. Have you seen Rex?" she called to Terrel.

Terrel swung Jason to the ground.

"Who are you?" the boy questioned. He didn't wait for an answer. "Will you play with me? I know where there's some rabbits."

"I saw the van come in," said Terrel, talking above his son's chatter. "Try the back garden."

Little Jason buzzed around them, pretending to be an airplane, then buzzed off after his father.

Megan, Peter, and Thuy followed Tonya along the driveway until they came to a big shed. Looking down a hill to the clearing beyond, Peter exclaimed, "Wow! That garden's big as a football field!"

Several people worked at the far end of the garden, too distant to see their faces.

"We feed lots of people here at Greentree Center all year round," said Tonya. "What we don't need, we sell in town."

In the shed, they saw a tractor and some other farm machines. Beside the tractor sat the brown van.

"Are you here, Rex?" Tonya called.

The tall young man Megan had seen at the store came around the corner of the shed with a shovel in his hand.

"Here. What's up?"

"Some visitors to see you."

Tonya smiled at them. "Nice talking to you. I'll leave you with Rex. I've got to get back to work." She left.

At last! The person who might know what happened to Dinh. Megan opened her mouth to introduce them, but Peter got right to the point. "Were you in Coupeville last Sunday?"

"Me?" Rex paused, thinking. "Yes. My wife and I took an emergency delivery of vegetables to one of the restaurants there. Why?"

"Did you give a ride to a boy about 17 years old?"

"Yes." He watched them, puzzled, as Thuy gave a soft cry. "Who wants to know?"

"He is my brother," Thuy said. "Please, where is he?"

Megan explained who they were and what had happened to Thuy and Dinh.

"The boy we picked up said his name was Jim. He said nothing about a boat or a sister ... or any trouble."

Thuy's lip began to quiver.

"Did he say his head hurt?" Peter asked quickly.

"No." Rex paused. "Didn't say much of anything, except that he needed to find work. He *did* seem dazed, out of it."

"Do you know where he went?"

"He's right here at Greentree," Rex said. He turned and pointed toward the garden below. "That's him, way down there, at the end of the field."

What Is the Matter
with Dinh?

Thuy's whole body went on tiptoe. "Let's go!"
Peter said.

But Megan held back. "Wait a minute," she said.
"There has to be a reason why Dinh went off like
that and why he hasn't told these people about Thuy or
the boat. We'd better move slowly until we find out why."

"You're right," Peter said. "Thuy, we'd better let you
talk to him by yourself first."

"All right," said Thuy. "But you'll go with me to the
garden, won't you?"

"Sure." They walked down the hill then along a path
that led through beds of carrots, bush beans, and other
vegetables. They passed several people working with
rakes and hoes. One skinny young man, with his hair in
a pony tail, straightened as they passed.

"Hi," he said, wiping his face with a bandanna.
"Looking for somebody?"

"Dinh," Peter said, gesturing toward the end of the
field.

"You mean Jim? Didn't know he had any friends."
The young man stuck the bandanna in his back pocket.

"Why do you say that?" Megan asked.

"He keeps pretty much to himself. Acts like he's got
lots of bad karma to deal with."

"Karma?" Peter repeated.

"You know ... things he did in previous lives that he's got to make up for now."

"Oh ... well, he's got friends," Peter told him. "Us. Thanks."

As they walked on, Megan said under her breath, "I've heard people talk about karma, but I just thought it was some kind of fad or catchword. That guy really believes it!"

"He seems to believe in reincarnation too," Peter said.

"My grandmother is Buddhist, you know," Thuy said. "She believes in reincarnation, I think. She doesn't talk about it, though."

"Well, it takes all kinds to make a world," Megan said. They came closer to the solitary figure picking something off potato plants and dropping it into a bucket.

"Is it Dinh, Thuy?" Megan asked.

"He looks different, but yes, it is him."

"This is far enough for us," Megan said. "Can you take it from here?"

Thuy nodded, eager and anxious at the same time.

The other two watched her walk toward a young man whose black hair looked like it hadn't been combed in days. His blue shirt was dirty and rumpled.

"What is he doing?" Megan asked.

"He's picking bugs off the plants, I think," Peter answered.

"Ugh!" Megan shivered. "I suppose if they don't use pesticides they have to fight the bugs some other way."

They watched Dinh stop working and stare as Thuy walked down the row toward him. He made no sign of recognition. Thuy stopped. She spoke, but Dinh just looked at her. He shook his head and stepped backward.

Megan and Peter moved closer to hear what they were saying. Thuy sounded ready to cry. "Don't you remember the Good Fortune? Or Grandmother? Don't you remember our home in Madrona Bay?"

"I live right here," the young man said. "I don't have a grandmother, or any other home. I don't have a sister." He shook his head as if trying to clear it. A confused, frightened expression flitted across his features. Then his face went blank, as if he'd pulled a shade across the emotions inside.

He turned and walked away. "My name is Jim," he said over his shoulder. "You've got me mixed up with someone else."

"Don't go. Please don't go, Dinh."

Megan thought she'd never heard a sadder voice as Thuy called after her brother. She and Peter hurried to their friend.

"Oh, Thuy, I'm so sorry." Megan put her arms around Thuy.

"Me too," said Peter, patting Thuy's shoulder. "What is wrong with him that he doesn't know his own sister?"

"Amnesia," Megan said. "Sometimes getting hit on the head can cause people to lose their memories. You see it all the time on TV."

"Maybe we'd better knock him on the head again to see if his memory comes back," Peter said.

Thuy looked at him, shocked.

"I'm kidding," he said hastily. "But even if he doesn't remember, he could have been nicer to you."

"There's nothing we can do right now," Megan said reluctantly. "It's late. If we don't get back, our parents will be worried sick."

"I can't go away and leave Dinh now that I've found him," cried Thuy.

"We can come back tomorrow," Peter told her. "Maybe one of the adults will know what to do next."

"Peter's right, Thuy," said Megan.

"Okay, but I don't want to go." As they walked through the garden, they stole glances over their shoulders. Dinh stood in the farthest corner, watching them. As they neared the shed, they saw him return to his work.

In the shed, Rex Hopner worked on the tractor. A slender woman with a long brown braid had joined him.

"Was he the one you're looking for?" Rex asked them.

"He is my brother," Thuy said. "But he doesn't know me."

"I'm not surprised," said the young woman. "He said so little about himself. Rex told me you said he'd been hurt. Sounds like a classic case of memory loss."

"This is my wife, Sandy," said Rex, introducing the young woman. "What are you going to do now?"

"We need to let our parents know where we are," said Megan. "Then I guess we'll go back to Coupeville."

"Don't worry, your brother is safe here," Sandy said to Thuy. To all of them, she said, "I'll take you back to the main building. You can use the telephone there if you like."

The trees cast long shadows across the lawn as they trooped after Sandy. She led them across the patio to the kitchen door and stuck her head inside. "Louann, will you show these people where the telephone is?"

"We don't all need to go in," said Megan. "Do you want to make the call, Peter?"

He fished in his pocket for the slip of paper with the restaurant's number. "Okay. Wait for me here."

"Hi, Sandy." Tonya and the other women who'd been working in the front garden came around the house to the patio and washed their hands at a faucet. "What do you think of Greentree Farm?" she asked the girls.

"It's beautiful," answered Thuy. "Very ... unusual."

"We're doing wonderful work here," said Tonya. "Work that will help to change the world."

Here was a chance to find out more about what these people believed. Megan probed, "It sounds like you're missionaries, in a way."

Tonya smiled. "In a way, we are. We're working to restore harmony between mankind and nature, between people and people."

Nothing wrong with that idea, Megan thought. After all, Jesus gave His life to bring us back to God. When God's Holy Spirit lives in our hearts, He changes them. What would Tonya say to that? She decided to find out. "I remember when I first began to realize how much God loved me. I looked at other people in a whole new way. And I appreciated God's world more too."

Tonya looked startled. "That's nice," she said.

Sandy glanced at Tonya, then turned to Megan and Thuy. "It was nice meeting you," she said. "I'm going to see what I can do to help Louann with the evening meal."

As Sandy went inside, good smells escaping

through the door made Megan realize that she was very hungry.

"I must get ready for supper," Tonya said. "Have a good evening." She followed the other women toward the cabins at the edge of the woods.

The shadow of the building had crept across the patio. The man with the shaven head half-opened his eyes and slowly unfolded from his cross-legged position by the lily pond. He stretched, then his eyes fastened on Megan. He started toward her.

"Oh, Peter, hurry up!" she exclaimed under her breath.

The man stopped very close. "I think I must have once been a cat," he said with a confidential smile. "I love to sit in the sun and meditate."

"Mmhmm," said Megan, stepping back and glancing over her shoulder. To her relief, Peter stood behind her.

"I love to get in touch with my higher self ... the Christ in me ... peace, joy, love ..."

"Oh, you're a Christian?" Peter asked, distracting the man's attention from Megan.

"I'm a Christian, a Buddhist, a Muslim—all are one, many paths lead to the same goal ..."

This guy is strange, Peter's expression read. Aloud he said, "What goal?"

"Enlightenment, perfection ... a new day is coming!"

"Did you know," asked Peter, surprising Megan with his boldness, "that Jesus says in the Bible, 'I am the way and the truth and the life. No one comes to the Father, except through Me'?"

The man's bare scalp glistened. His lips continued

to smile, but his eyes narrowed as he looked at Peter. "Jesus was a great teacher. Everyone knows that."

Peter took a deep breath. "Yes, but do you believe that Jesus died for you and came alive again?"

The man did not answer his challenge.

"Jesus did that for you, you know. Believing in Jesus as your Savior is what being a Christian is all about."

Though the smile stayed glued to the man's face, his eyes slid away from Peter's. He raised his hands in the air. "Peace ... joy ... love ..." he chanted as he walked away.

"Oh, Peter. You were wonderful!" said Megan, and she meant it. "Something about that fellow makes me very uncomfortable."

Thuy gave Peter an admiring glance. "Me too," she said. "I want to get my brother away from here as soon as possible."

"Speaking of getting away from here ..." Megan began.

"Our parents were in the restaurant eating when I called," Peter said. "They were pretty worried. They said they'll wait on the wharf for us. And they'll buy us dinner when we get there."

Megan's stomach rumbled. "I can hardly wait!"

"But what about Dinh?" Thuy asked.

"They're trying to think of something," Peter explained. "We'll all come back tomorrow. Oh, yes, they promised to call your grandmother right away so she'll know that Dinh is safe."

"Oh, good!" Thuy's eyes shone with unshed tears. "This has been very hard for her."

"It's been hard for you too," Megan told Thuy as they walked around to the front of the building. "But soon you and Dinh will be safely home again."

Little Jason played in the tire swing beneath the big Madrona tree as they went past. His father raked dead leaves, leathery and brown, and bits of shed bark into a pile.

"I went up and petted your doggie," Jason announced.

"Thanks," said Peter. "Jiggs probably thinks we forgot about him."

"I told him you'd be back," said the little boy. "Didn't I, Terrel?" He trotted in circles around his father, stamping on ants that had been disturbed by the leaf rake.

"Jason," the father said. "The ants are our little brothers. We don't want to hurt them."

He leaned on his rake. "You found Rex?" he asked the three.

"Yes, we did. Thank you."

They passed the garden and crossed the wooden bridge. Jiggs' wagging tail almost propelled him through the open window as he greeted them.

"I'll take him for a run along the driveway while you're turning around," Peter said to Megan. "You can pick us up."

She nodded and slid behind the steering wheel. Peter let his dog out and raced away toward the woods with him.

After his long afternoon of waiting in the van, Jiggs could hardly contain his exuberance. Megan saw him plow through the sword fern, stop to explore interesting scents, then zigzag crazily through the trees. His barking faded as Megan tried the ignition. The engine turned over, sputtered, and died. She tried again with the same results, several times, then got out and raised the hood. Thuy joined her, looking worried.

Peter came back to the clearing. "I wondered where you were. What's wrong?"

Megan lifted her head from beneath the hood. "It won't go. Did you ..."

Peter raised his hand in the scout's oath. "Not this time. I didn't touch it." He joined the girls in staring into the engine compartment. "Does it start at all?"

"Listen." Megan got back in and turned the key. The engine turned over, coughed, choked, and stopped.

"Uh-oh," said Peter. "I'll bet it's the fuel pump."

"Maybe somebody here can fix it," Thuy suggested.

Terrel and his little boy walked up to them. Peter told him what he thought was wrong. "I'll get Rex," Terrel said. "He knows more about engines than I do."

While they waited, the sun dipped to the treetops on the far side of the lake. The air grew cooler. Megan thought longingly of their dinner waiting in Coupeville.

Finally Terrel returned with Rex. The two men bent over the engine. Megan again attempted to start it.

"It's the fuel pump, all right," said Rex. "We don't have a replacement here that will fit, either."

"Oh no!" wailed Megan. "Our parents are waiting for us in Coupeville. Our truck is at Fort Ebey. They can't even come get us!"

"Can you call them?"

"They're probably still at the restaurant," said Peter. "We can try."

Rex gave Jiggs a pat. "Bring your dog. Maybe Louann has a soup bone she can give him."

As they walked down the hill, Peter whispered to the girls, "If we don't eat soon, I'm going to ask Louann for a soup bone for me!"

They left Jiggs outside the back door while the girls followed Peter to the phone in an alcove off the kitchen. In the room beyond, several of the people they'd seen working in the gardens sat eating.

Peter dialed. "Hello. This is Peter Lewis. Is this Jen? I talked to you a little while ago, Jen, and asked to speak to my parents. Are they still in the restaurant?"

He waited while the waitress went to look. "They're not? If they come back, would you have them call us at the Greentree Farm? It's important."

He gave the waitress the number and replaced the receiver. "They're gone."

Megan knew she must look as worried as Peter and Thuy, but she said, "They'll be back. They said they'd wait for us."

"But when will they be back?" muttered Peter. "And what can they do to help, even then? Like you said, we've got the van, and they're on foot."

A Long Day

Louann, the cook, walking by with a basket of hot corn muffins, noticed their downcast faces. "Would something to eat cheer you up?"

Peter sniffed appreciatively. "Would it ever," he said. "We can't get in touch with our parents. It might be midnight before we get back to Coupeville."

"Come sit down. I'll set you some places." She showed them to an empty table in the dining room and brought some dishes, a serving bowl brimming with homemade soup, and some muffins. "Now, if you're all set, may I feed your dog some scraps? I heard him whimpering outside the door."

"Thanks," Peter said. "He'll be your friend for life."

"Shall we each ask our own blessing?" asked Megan, glancing at the people still eating and talking at the other tables. They bowed their heads, then served themselves.

They ate ravenously. Although the soup contained mostly vegetables, it tasted wonderful. Peter dipped himself some more and buttered another muffin.

"Dinh is not here," whispered Thuy.

"Maybe not everyone eats here," Megan told her. "I don't see Terrel and little Jason either."

"There's your friend with the shiny head." Peter grinned at Megan, nodding toward a table in the corner.

The man who loved to meditate seemed to be preaching to several people they'd not seen before.

Megan shuddered and sipped a spoonful of soup. She hoped Darren or her mother would call soon. Would they be angry? She didn't think they'd blame her for whatever was wrong with the fuel pump, but Mom hadn't been real happy with them going off on their own. Now she'd think her protectiveness was justified. And Darren would probably side with Mom.

They finished eating and carried their bowls and spoons to the kitchen where several people rinsed and stacked dishes, then immersed them in a deep sink of sudsy water.

"May we do anything?" Megan asked.

"We've got plenty of helpers," Louann told them. "Why don't you just relax and enjoy yourselves until our leader arrives to give tonight's lecture?"

"You listen to lectures at night?" Peter's voice betrayed his opinion that sitting through a lecture was the last thing he'd choose to do in the evening.

Louann glanced at him, amused. "Quite often we do. Our leader feels we have much to learn, and our days are busy with the work of the farm."

The young people returned to the big room where they'd eaten. People were shoving tables against the wall and arranging chairs in semicircles.

Megan inspected a collection of quartz crystals in a glass case against the wall. "Aren't they beautiful?" she said to the others. "Some people think they're magical. I wonder if these people think that?"

Just then, several people came into the room, distracting their attention. Megan recognized the first as the man with thick glasses from the "Save the Planet" booth at the Langley street fair.

She tried not to stare at the tall, slightly stooped man who came next. Silver hair framed a long face whose flesh sagged like softening wax. Pale eyes swept the room, pausing a moment to examine the three young people, then swept on. His deep voice reverberated as if he were talking into a barrel. "Let it be known," he proclaimed. "We are ready to begin."

Tonya, the gardener and bookstore clerk, hurried across the room to greet their leader.

"I see we have guests," he rumbled.

"Yes, temporary guests," Tonya explained. "They are waiting for help with their car." The man gazed piercingly at each one as she introduced them. "Megan, Thuy, Peter, this is our teacher and leader, Chandrat Lansing."

Megan offered her hand. "How do you do?"

"Welcome." The man turned abruptly away, as if he'd not noticed her outstretched hand, and moved to a single chair facing the semicircles. He sat down, folded his hands in his lap, and closed his eyes. Tonya turned down the lights and went back to the kitchen.

He didn't move, not even an eyelid, as more people slipped into the room. Megan caught the eyes of the others and gestured toward three seats near the door.

"Creepy," Peter mouthed to Megan. She nodded agreement and took the chair on the end.

When the rustle of people seating themselves died away, Chandrat Lansing slowly raised his head. His pale gaze slid from face to face as he stood.

Out of the corner of her eye, Megan saw Dinh slip into the room. Peter saw him too and nudged Thuy. But Dinh avoided looking in their direction.

Then Lansing's powerful voice filled the room with its hypnotic rumble. "Our perpetual questions, friends, are these: How can we best participate in advancing the evolution of human culture? And, how can we protect the planet on which we live?"

I'll go along with the second question, Megan thought. Who could argue with the need for taking care of the earth? But she wasn't sure what the leader meant by his first question.

"Here at Greentree Farm, we learn to honor, understand, and respect the spirit that moves in all things. We seek to find our own spiritual power and so become change agents for a better world."

Peter glanced at Megan. She raised her eyebrows, letting him know this sounded peculiar to her too. A telephone rang in the kitchen.

A moment later, Tonya came out, touched Megan's shoulder, and beckoned her to follow. Good, Megan thought as she got up. Their parents must have received Peter's message. Tonya quietly closed the door and busied herself at the other end of the room as Megan picked up the phone.

Darren's voice answered her hello. "Are you all right, Megan? What's happened?"

She told her stepfather about the broken fuel pump. Silence. He *was* angry, just as she'd feared. Finally Darren spoke, his voice betraying nothing but relief.

"Just so you're all okay. But we do have a problem. It's nearly eight o'clock on a Sunday night. I doubt anyone here would have the right part, even if we found a place open. And your Mom and I are stuck without transportation!"

Megan swallowed hard. This had been her idea in the first place. "I'm sorry. What should we do?"

"Will the people at the farm let you stay there until morning? Is there anyone I can talk to?"

Megan signaled Tonya. She quickly told her the problem and handed her the phone.

"Yes, Mr. Lewis. We'll find sleeping quarters for them. They'll be fine here." She gave directions to the farm, then handed the phone back to Megan.

"Megan," her stepfather said in a low voice, "I wish we didn't have to leave you there, but we'll come just as soon as we can. Be sure you all stay together."

"We will. Darren ... thanks."

Back in the big room, Megan noticed Dinh was no longer in his seat. The remaining listeners hung on Chandrat Lansing's every word as his voice rumbled on. In the dim light, Thuy and Peter turned to her. She gestured toward the door.

They tiptoed outside and moved away from the building. Jiggs, who'd been waiting in the yard, woofed happily, and Peter quickly shushed him. A football shaped moon skimmed the top of the Madrona tree.

"We have to stay here tonight. They can't get a fuel pump this late."

"I was afraid of that," Peter said.

"Do we have to sleep in the van?" Thuy asked.

"Tonya said they had room for us. But maybe Jiggs should sleep in the van to guard it," Megan suggested.

They made their way along the moonlit driveway to the minivan. Megan unlocked the door.

Peter retrieved Megan's camera and gave it to her before he told Jiggs to jump in. The dog circled three times on the floor between the seats and dropped with a grunt.

"He's tired," Thuy said and sighed. "So am I."

"I'm tired too," said Megan. "But we can't find a place to sleep with everybody sitting there listening to those peculiar ideas. This is the weirdest experience I've ever had."

"Me too," said Peter. "Don't you think we ought to pray that God will work everything out for us?"

"Yes," said Megan, ashamed that she'd not suggested it herself. She reached out her hands to Thuy and Peter to make a circle. "Shall I go first? Dear God," she prayed, "You know we feel uncomfortable here. I don't know why we do, but we ask You to protect us tonight."

"And Father," Peter added, "please help Dinh to remember who he is."

"And take care of our parents and Thuy's grandmother too," Megan added. "In Jesus' name. Amen."

"Amen," said Thuy. "Thank you. What shall we do now?"

Peter looked toward the lake glimmering in the moonlight. "Do you think there's a path to the water?"

"While we were in the garden and Thuy was talking to Dinh, I saw a road that went in that direction," Megan answered.

Thuy hitched her knapsack to her shoulders. "I wish we could find Dinh. I want to talk to him again."

"Maybe he's back in the meeting." They peered through the windows of the big house as they skirted it in the moonlight, but they didn't see Dinh. "It's like they're hypnotized by that man Lansing," Megan whispered.

"It's funny," Peter answered. "What he says almost makes sense ... but there's something wrong."

"I think I know what it is," Megan said. "While he was talking I sort of had the feeling those people are looking inside themselves for power ... to change themselves, to change the world. But only God has that power. And He gives it to us through His Holy Spirit."

"That's it!" Peter said. "Remember Adam and Eve? When the devil told them, 'you'll be like God if you eat the fruit,' instead of obeying God."

Thuy listened intently as Megan said, "It's as if these people want to be like God, but they don't want to do it God's way."

They walked across the grassy area where big trees cast pools of black shadow. One or two lights shone from the little buildings at the forest's edge.

"Dinh could be in one of those cottages," Thuy said.

"Could be," Peter answered. "But we'd better not go knocking on doors at this time of night."

They passed the big garden and followed a lane through the moonlit meadow. Tire ruts led to a marshy beach. A dock jutted into the lake. Grass and sedges grew along the water's edge; light-barked alder trees rimmed the lake beyond the meadow.

They walked onto the dock. Peter took off his sneakers and socks and dangled his feet in the water. "It's warm!" he exclaimed. "I wish we had our swimsuits!"

Megan kicked off her shoes and stepped into the shallow water. The muddy bottom squished ooze between her toes. She waded back to the others and splashed her feet in the water to rinse them. "When we set out for Whidbey Island three days ago," she said, slapping at a mosquito buzzing her ear, "who would have thought we'd end up stranded in a place like this?"

"It's my fault. You wouldn't be here if you hadn't tried to help me." Thuy dropped her forehead against her knees.

"Don't be a nut," Peter said. "When we're all safely home again, we'll look back and think we had a great adventure."

Thuy raised her head with a wry smile. "It's an adventure. But except for meeting you two, it's not great."

Megan stared into the night. Along the margin of the lake, the alder trunks made pale streaks against the dark evergreens. Suddenly she stiffened. "Stay just as you are, everybody. Something moved in those trees. Someone's watching us."

"Probably just a deer," said Peter.

"No. A person."

"Maybe it's Dinh," Thuy said.

"On the chance it is Dinh, why don't you move to the end of the dock, where he can see you better," Peter suggested to her. "Play your flute for him."

"Oh, that's a wonderful idea!" Thuy took her flute

from her knapsack and walked to the end of the dock. She raised the instrument to her lips.

Softly the notes rang out, first something that sounded faintly Oriental, then the Mozart piece.

Megan lay down on her stomach and pillowed her head on her arms. Perhaps whoever lurked in the forest would not realize she watched for another glimpse of movement. The air became cool, and the mosquitoes bolder. Thuy played until she grew tired, but Megan saw no one. "Either he's gone or he doesn't want us to know he's there," she said.

"Yes, and I see more lights up at the farm," said Peter. "The lecture must be over. We'd better find out where we sleep tonight."

"Your dad said we should stay together," Megan told him. "But I really don't think these people are dangerous. Do you?"

"No," said Peter. "Aside from their strange ideas, they seem pretty nice. But we should do what Dad said anyway."

At the big house, a few of the men put the tables and chairs back in place for breakfast next morning. Louann and Tonya came out of the kitchen as the young people entered the front door.

"We wondered what happened to you," Louann said. "Are you ready to turn in? We get up early here."

"We don't want to put you to any trouble ..." Megan began.

"It's no trouble. Peter, you can bunk with a couple of the fellows. Tonya will take one of you girls with her, and there's an extra bed for the other in my room here

133

in the big building."

"Couldn't we just sleep on the floor in this room?" Peter suggested.

"Nonsense. That would be very uncomfortable."

The three glanced at one another helplessly. Louann had it all worked out. Besides, they weren't in a position to protest the arrangements.

The pony-tailed young man from the garden put the last chair in place and walked over to the group. "Ready to go, Peter?"

"All right. See you in the morning," Peter said to the girls as he followed the young man onto the porch. Megan watched Peter start across the lawn, wishing she could think of a way to keep them all together.

Suddenly the sound of an engine came from the forest. Headlights slashed the darkness. They heard Jiggs bark as a vehicle pulled into the parking lot.

"That sounds like Dad's truck!" Peter yelled. He whirled and raced toward the parking lot. "Dad!" he called.

"Right here," came his father's voice. "Are you okay? Where are the girls?"

Megan and Thuy ran up to the truck. "We're here," Megan panted. "Where's Mom?"

"How did you get the truck, Dad?" Peter queried.

"We found my brother. We found my brother!" Thuy exclaimed.

Darren laughed at the barrage of words. "Sarah stayed at camp. And yes, Thuy, we know you found Dinh. Your friend gave good directions, Megan. I came right here, though I must admit I wondered where I'd end up when I started the drive through the woods."

Tonya and Louann waited in the open doorway of the big house as Darren walked down with the young people to introduce himself. "Thank you for taking care of the kids. When the cook at the restaurant gave us a ride back to Fort Ebey, I realized I could probably get here before you all went to bed. I'll take them with me, and we'll come back tomorrow to get the van, if that's all right."

"That's fine," said Louann. "We'll see you tomorrow."

Back at the truck, Darren handed them the jackets he'd brought along. Megan slipped hers on, glad for its warmth. She and Thuy climbed into the cab while Peter boosted Jiggs into the back of the pickup and made himself comfortable against the rolled up sleeping bags his father had tossed in.

As the truck bumped through the dark forest toward the highway, Megan sighed. They'd sleep safely in their own camp tonight. And they'd found Dinh. But the almost inaudible sniffle beside her told her that for Thuy, Dinh was still lost. What could they do about that?

Danger!

When Megan woke the next morning, the sun had already begun to burn through the fog. She peered out her tent flap to see her mother and stepfather talking quietly at the picnic table.

Thuy opened sleepy eyes.

"Morning," Megan yawned. She squirmed into clean clothes before leaving the warmth of her sleeping bag, then grabbed her shoes and socks and crawled out of the tent.

"Good morning!" Mom lit the burners of the camp stove. "How many hot cakes for you?"

"Lots." Megan thought of the bowl of soup she'd had for supper last night. "I could eat a whole batch myself!"

Megan had just started in on her first plateful when Thuy came to the table. Then Peter poked his head out of his tent. Sarah Lewis flipped hotcakes and scrambled eggs. As they ate, they described Greentree Farm and its inhabitants in detail and filled Sarah in on what had happened the day before.

"We need to get back to the farm as soon as possible, but I'll have to go to Oak Harbor for the fuel pump ... they have several parts stores there," Darren said. "Megan, why don't you let me take your film to one of those quick-print places while I'm there? I don't know how we'll persuade Dinh to leave the farm, but at least your pictures of his assailants and their boat might help the sheriff track them down."

"Especially since Dinh was injured badly enough to cause loss of memory," said Sarah. "Don't you think they're liable for charges of assault?"

"They should be ... no question about it," said Darren.

Thuy looked from one adult to another. "I just want my brother to come home. I want to see him smile again."

"We want him home too," said Darren. "I'm not sure what group operates Greentree Farm, but the things you kids saw and heard tell us they are not teaching truth. I'd hate to see Dinh get sucked into a cult."

They sat for a few minutes planning the day. First, everyone would pack his or her own duffle bag and help to put the campsite in order. Then, with everything ready to go, Darren and Sarah would leave the others in Coupeville and go on to Oak Harbor.

From Oak Harbor, the adults would go directly to Greentree Farm so Darren could install the fuel pump, then bring the van back, after trying again to talk to Dinh. Then they'd retrieve the Good Fortune and the Lewis' boat from the wharf in Coupeville and head back to Madrona Bay.

"What are we supposed to do in Coupeville while you're gone?" Megan asked.

"You can collect the posters you put up around town. Maybe you'd like to spend some time at the museum or do some window-shopping."

"Window-shopping? No way!" exclaimed Peter.

"Maybe we can take the Good Fortune out and be sure it's ready for the run back to Madrona Bay," Thuy suggested.

Peter brightened. "Yeah!"

Megan and Peter finished their share of the cleanup quickly. Thuy, of course, had very little to pack. "Do we have time to take Jiggs over to the bunker for a run?" Peter asked his stepmother.

"Go ahead. But don't be gone long."

They ran along the path that led past Thuy's old camp, past the gun emplacements and bunker of Fort Ebey. Peter let Jiggs run free on the meadow overlooking the Straits of Juan de Fuca while the three young people walked to the edge of the bluff.

Across the sparkling water, the tiny buildings of Port Townsend looked sharp and clear in the morning sun. "May I ask a question?" Thuy said. "Last night, Megan, you said those people at the farm want to be like God, but they're not doing it God's way. What did you mean?"

"Oh," Megan said, "I guess I meant that through their own efforts they are trying to become like God. And that's impossible. Human beings are just naturally sinful, no matter how good they try to be."

"So what is God's way?"

"I can answer that," Peter said. "God's way was to send Jesus, His Son, to live the perfect life we can't live and to die for our sins."

"Mine too?"

"Yes," Megan told her. "God sends His Holy Spirit to live in us. He helps us to be sorry for our sins and to believe that Jesus died in our place. Then when God looks at us, He sees what Jesus did for us instead of seeing our sins. And the Holy Spirit helps us live like He wants us to live."

"Really?" said Thuy. "Would He do that for me too?"

"Do you believe that Jesus died for you?" Megan asked her.

"Yes," Thuy nodded slowly. "I do."

"Then let's tell Him so," Megan smiled.

The three of them bowed their heads while Thuy thanked Jesus for dying for her sins and for making her part of God's family.

It had all happened so unexpectedly that even after Thuy and Peter ran with Jiggs back toward camp, Megan felt dazed. "God, this is wonderful!" she whispered. "Thank You! Thank You for bringing us to Whidbey. Thank You for bringing us together with Thuy. And thank You for the way I know You'll answer our prayers for Dinh!"

~~~~~~~~~~~~

Megan arrived at the campsite in time to hear Thuy shyly tell the adults, "I belong to Jesus, just like you."

Sarah swung around from the picnic table, joy shining from her face. "How wonderful, Thuy!"

"I can't wait to tell Dinh," Thuy said. "I hope he'll listen!"

"Well," said Darren, "we'll do what we can for Dinh. But first, let's take time to thank God for what He's done for Thuy and to ask Him to guide us and help us today."

They stood in a circle while they prayed. Then Peter boosted Jiggs into the back of the truck and climbed in after him. Thuy and Megan piled in with Peter, the adults got in the front, and they were off to Coupeville.

First stop was the sheriff's office. Darren went in and came right out. "All the officers are busy on the highways since it's Labor Day," he reported. "No one's there until eleven."

"It's not even ten yet," said Sarah. "We'll have to come back."

"We can walk to the shops from here," Megan said.

"Shall Sarah and I take Jiggs with us?" Peter's dad asked him.

"He'd probably be happier," Peter answered. He fastened the leash to the pickup bed so that Jiggs could lie down or move around, but not fall over the edge. "Don't forget to give him water."

"We'll take care of him," Darren Lewis answered, rumpling his son's windblown hair. "We'll be back with both vehicles this afternoon, if all goes well."

"Sounds good," answered Peter. "Did you give them your film, Megan?"

She nodded, patting her camera. "I put another roll in this morning."

Jiggs barked as the pickup pulled away from the three on the sidewalk. They walked downhill to the town's short main street. Already tourists wandered in and out of the shops. Megan, Peter, and Thuy wandered in and out too, collecting fliers they'd left before.

"Look at all the boats," Megan commented as they came to the wharf. "There's ours, on the far side of the floats."

"Where's the Good Fortune?" Thuy asked, a note of

141

panic in her voice. Then she laughed. "I see it. Behind that big boat."

"Looks like lots of people are enjoying the official last day of summer," Megan said. "Tomorrow everybody goes back to work."

"Or to school," said Peter, making a face.

They paused when they reached the restaurant on the wharf to look down at the Nguyen's trim little gray and white boat.

Thuy clutched Peter's arm. "Somebody's aboard," she whispered.

"How do you know?" asked Peter. "I don't see anybody."

"Something moved."

"We'd better not go down without help," Megan said. "Someone could be trying to steal the boat. Maybe even someone with a gun."

"The Good Fortune belongs to me and my brother," said Thuy. "I'm going to see who's there."

She squeezed past some people who were coming up from the floats, then, holding on to the chain railings, she marched down the gangplank.

"Wait a minute, Thuy," Peter said as he and Megan hurried to catch up. "There're lots of people around. I don't think there'll be any trouble. But let me go aboard first."

He jumped onto the deck of the Good Fortune. With a hazy idea of getting the evidence on film in case someone was prowling, Megan aimed her camera and shot. Peter looked through a porthole into the low cabin, then beckoned to Thuy, who hopped aboard and looked through the same window.

Thuy gave a glad cry and disappeared into the cabin. "It's Dinh," Peter told Megan.

After a few minutes, Thuy stuck her head out the door. "Everybody, come here!"

They crowded into the small cabin where Thuy stood beside her brother. He was dressed in clean clothing, his hair neatly combed. "Dinh's back!" she said happily. "He remembers!"

Dinh's smile spread from ear to ear as his sister introduced her friends. "Peter and Megan found me at Fort Ebey, Dinh, and they and their family invited me to camp with them. And they've helped me look for you ever since."

"I can't believe this!" Megan said. "How did you get here? When did your memory come back?"

"Sit down, please," said Dinh. "I will tell you what happened."

They found places to sit.

"When I saw you at the farm, I felt very confused," he began.

"When Thuy tried to talk to me it seemed that she was telling a story about someone else. Then last night when I was at the lake, you came to the dock. When I heard Thuy play her flute, bits of memory began to come back, like scraps of photographs blown by the wind ... I couldn't make sense of them."

Dinh grinned widely. "When you left, I went to bed, but the pictures kept coming, clearer and clearer. Suddenly I remembered the fight on the wharf, and then everything came back. So I got up, hiked to the road, and caught a ride to Coupeville. I found our boat and fell asleep. I was just wondering how I would find you."

"Oh, Dinh, I'm so glad you're here!" Thuy's smile matched Dinh's. "Let's call Grandmother and tell her you're all right."

"Yes," answered Dinh. "We'll call her and tell her we're coming home, after I thank your parents for taking care of Thuy, of course," he said to Megan and Peter. "Then let's take the boat for a ride, to be sure everything is working properly."

Peter explained what their parents were doing. "But we could go for a ride," he said. "Thuy wanted to take the boat out anyway."

Thuy jumped up and searched her pockets for a quarter. "I'll go call Grandmother right now!"

"Let me do it," said Dinh. "I think she'll feel better if I tell her myself that my memory is back."

"Okay. But I'll go with you." Brother and sister left to use the pay phone.

Sitting on the Good Fortune's deck, legs dangling over the side, Megan and Peter watched them go.

Peter glanced sideways at Megan. "Dinh's lucky to have a sister like Thuy. Would you have worried about me like that if I'd been the one who was lost?"

"We've been friends a long time. Of course I would worry."

"But I'm your brother now ... stepbrother, anyway. Does that make a difference?"

Megan felt a twinge of irritation. What did he want her to say? Then her thoughts skipped back over the past several days ... Peter's patience with her moods, his kindness to Thuy. Peter really tried to live what he said

144

he believed. And that had made a life-changing difference to Thuy.

"Just because our parents got married doesn't mean you and I automatically have a brother-sister relationship. But," she told him honestly, "if I could have chosen any brother I wanted, he'd be a lot like you."

Peter grinned. "That's good enough for me."

Thuy and Dinh came back smiling at their grandmother's reaction to their news. Dinh tried the Good Fortune's motor. It coughed a few times, then started. He handed life jackets to each of them, then popped a section of the cabin roof out of the way so he could stand with his head and shoulders through the opening while he steered.

Peter jumped onto the dock to release the lines that held the boat, then leaped back aboard. They were off.

The girls sat aft where they could watch the wake foaming behind them. Peter sat on the cabin roof, holding to the low railing around it, while Dinh steered the Good Fortune down Penn Cove. They passed the city launch ramp, then went by the places where they'd searched for the missing boat three days ago.

Finally they passed through the entrance to Penn Cove and followed the shore to the point where they'd found the Good Fortune aground.

"It's a good thing the hull did not cave in against those logs," Dinh said.

By now Megan and Peter had told Dinh about meeting the crew of the Sister Susie in Langley. "Thuy identified them. We have all the information if you want to press charges for assault," Megan said.

Dinh shrugged. "What good would it do? I am just happy to have my sister safe and my boat back."

"Well, for one thing," Peter replied, "they might think twice before they pick on someone."

Dinh swung the boat farther into the waters of Saratoga Passage, preparing to turn back into Penn Cove. As he did so, the motor sputtered. Then it died.

The boat rocked, drifting with the current that flowed into the cove as Dinh tried to restart it. Peter jumped off the cabin roof and went below to see if he could help. Megan, too, crowded inside while Thuy watched from the doorway.

"We're drifting toward a deadhead," she reported, sounding worried.

Megan looked out the nearest porthole. Still some distance away, but in line with their direction of drift, she saw what Thuy was talking about ... a waterlogged tree or stump. Only a small part showed above the water. The rest, like an iceberg, hung dangerously out of sight below the surface.

Dinh worked harder with the motor. It sputtered once or twice, then died again. Wind blew them closer to the deadhead bobbing in the water. Megan couldn't tell exactly where below the surface the rest of it lay, but the waves occasionally lifted enough of it above the water that she could see it was big. Who could tell what jagged branches might lie below the water line, waiting to spear whatever collided with it?

"Do you have any more gas?" Peter asked. "Maybe there's moisture in the fuel lines."

"Behind you, in that cupboard."

Peter bent over and found the gas can in the compartment. He handed it to Dinh, who carefully splashed some into the carburetor.

Thuy turned from the deadhead to stare in the opposite direction, toward Saratoga Passage. "Oh, no!" she exclaimed.

Megan leaped to the other side of the cabin and looked through another porthole. "It's the Sister Susie," she gasped.

She saw the squat form of the man called Buffalo aim a pair of binoculars in their direction. He dropped them and pointed. A flurry of activity erupted on the Sister Suzie's deck, then she altered course and accelerated, heading straight toward them.

"Look out," Megan screamed. "They're going to ram us!"

Castaways No Longer

The bobbing deadhead drew steadily nearer as the current pushed the Good Fortune along. "The anchor!" Megan shouted. "Should we throw out the anchor?" But even as she shrieked the words, she knew they were trapped. The Sister Susie bore directly toward them. If the deadhead didn't get them, the Sister Susie would.

"They must be crazy!" Peter exploded. He dashed for the deck, yelling and waving his arms. Megan and Thuy rushed after him and yelled too, while Dinh frantically worked over the motor.

The other boat slowed momentarily when the men aboard saw the extra passengers, then accelerated again.

"They're trying to hit us!" Thuy screamed.

The motor coughed and turned over. "Hold on," Peter shouted to the girls. The Sister Susie was almost upon them. Dinh again yanked the starter. The motor sputtered, then caught. Dinh gave it full throttle. The Good Fortune leaped ahead as if kicked from behind.

As the big pleasure craft roared past their stern, Megan glimpsed fury on Ole's hatchet face. She heard one of the women scream "Look out!" and saw Buffalo's glare of hatred turn to utter terror as he jerked forward and saw the deadhead.

"They're going to crash!" Peter cried.

Buffalo spun the Sister Susie's wheel frantically. For a moment it seemed they would miss the deadhead. Then came a solid *whump*. At the same instant the boat heaved to starboard and almost capsized. Passengers tumbled across the deck and landed against the bulkhead. Sister Susie's engine screeched into silence. Momentum carried her a few yards farther, then she slid to a halt, as dead in the water as the Good Fortune had been moments earlier.

Dinh let his engine idle as he steered the Good Fortune close to the Sister Susie. The people aboard lay in a heap, limp and unbelieving.

"Will they sink?" Megan asked.

"I don't think so," answered Dinh. "The hull just scraped the deadhead. But look at their propeller!"

Megan stared. The smashed propeller and shaft assembly bent up out of the water at a useless angle. Their motor was probably damaged too. Buffalo and his friends wouldn't get back to land under their own power.

Another boat which had been nearby was heading toward the Good Fortune. It drew abreast and a brawny man called, "I saw what happened. Are you all right?"

"Yes," Dinh called back. "We are fine." To Peter he said, "Toss that rope at the stern to the Sister Susie. We will tow them in." Dinh's smile had vanished.

"Will you press charges now?" Megan asked.

Dinh nodded. "You bet."

Peter fastened the end of the rope to the stern, then coiled and tossed it through the air. The other end landed on the deck of the Sister Susie.

Neither Ole nor Buffalo made any effort to grab it. "We

don't need your help," snarled Buffalo. "Get out of here."

"You guys better accept their help," yelled the man from the other boat. "I'm radioing ahead to the harbor master. There's no way you're going to get by with what you tried to do."

Buffalo glared and didn't move. But as the other boat moved closer, he took a second look at its brawny pilot and made the rope fast to the prow of his boat. "I was only trying to scare them," he growled.

"I'll follow you in," the pilot called to the young people. "And I'll testify against these hoodlums in court, if necessary."

"Thank you," they called back. Slowly, Dinh accelerated while the rope grew taut. His little boat chugged through the waters of Penn Cove. The pleasure craft wallowed behind while its four passengers clutched the rails and sulked.

Thuy and Peter stood at the prow of the Good Fortune. Megan perched nearby on the roof of the cabin.

"When I first saw the Sister Susie out there, I prayed," she heard Thuy tell Peter. "And God heard me!"

"I'm glad," Peter answered. "God always answers His children's prayers. Sometimes not the way we think He will. But He always does. What did you pray?"

"I just said, in my head, 'God help!' He *did* help, didn't He?"

"He sure did," Peter said. "And He helped us find Dinh, and He brought Dinh's memory back."

The two stood silent for a few moments, watching the bow wave foaming past. Megan barely heard what

Thuy said next.

"Peter, when we're both busy in our classes at Madrona High next year, will you still be my friend?"

Peter bent his bright head to look into Thuy's sparkling eyes. "I'll be proud to be your friend," he answered. "You are one of the bravest people I know."

Megan cleared her throat. "Something's happening on the wharf," she said, pointing.

Police cars with flashing lights, an ambulance, even a fire truck, were lined up along the wharf. Crowds of onlookers spilled down the bluff and onto the beach. Men in uniform stood on the floats.

The boater who'd appointed himself their escort pulled alongside to call, "They're waiting for you. Go ahead, bring in your prisoners." He seemed to be enjoying this.

Megan spotted her mom and Peter's dad at the railing near the restaurant. She waved as Dinh cut the motor and let the Good Fortune nose into a place against the forward float.

Soon, officers swarmed aboard the Sister Susie to handcuff all four of its passengers and read them their rights.

"But we didn't have anything to do with this," he heard one of the women wail as she wobbled away in her skimpy outfit and high heels.

As soon as Buffalo, Ole, and the women were safely in the patrol cars, Darren and Sarah Lewis rushed down to the float. Megan's mom hugged her and Peter and Thuy. Both adults shook hands with Dinh as Thuy introduced them. They asked more questions than could possibly be answered all at once.

The sheriff cut into the excited conversation. "We'll need these four to come to the station to give their statements."

Megan looked for their brawny friend and beckoned him over.

"I saw everything that happened," the man told the sheriff.

"Will you give us a statement?"

"Glad to. People like that shouldn't be allowed on the water. Why would they risk the lives of a bunch of kids?"

Megan looked at Dinh and Thuy. Yes, why? she wondered. How could anybody hate people they didn't even know?

~~~~~~~~~~~~~~~~~~~~~~~~

In the sheriff's crowded office, Peter, Thuy, and Megan stood against the wall while Dinh gave his statement.

"You know," said Thuy, "I don't hate those men ... Buffalo and Ole ... anymore. I feel sorry for them."

Megan met Peter's glance. "That's God's Holy Spirit living in your heart now," she said. "Not that we don't get mad anymore when somebody wrongs us, but Jesus says we should forgive them, and He helps us do it."

"I wish I could tell them about Jesus," Thuy mused.

"For a brand-new Christian, you're learning fast," Megan said, feeling ashamed that she hadn't had the same thought. "We can pray for them, anyhow."

Finally they finished in the sheriff's office and gathered outside with Darren and Sarah.

"I'm starving," Peter said. "Is it lunchtime yet?"

His father glanced at his watch and laughed. "It's two o'clock. No wonder you're hungry."

They checked to be sure Jiggs was all right in the pickup, then walked down the hill to the shops. "I saw an interesting place along here this morning that serves homemade chowder and bakery goods," Megan's mother said. "Yes, here it is."

A sign on one of the old buildings on the bluff pointed them down some steps to a lower entrance. Inside, windows with ruffled curtains overlooked Penn Cove and the wharf. They seated themselves at two small rustic tables.

"Order whatever you want," Darren said. "This will be our last meal out for a long time. Tonight we'll eat supper at home."

Thuy smiled at her brother. "Home. It sounds wonderful."

Megan's mind had darted elsewhere, jarred by her stepfather's words. She'd almost forgotten she'd be going back to a strange new house, living every day with two extra people. She glanced past Thuy at her mother and Darren, sitting side by side at the other table. Mom looked happier and more relaxed than Megan could ever remember. Even if her own father had come back, could he have made Mom that happy? She and Peter and Darren and her mom had worked together like a real family to help Thuy find Dinh. Maybe this whole blended-family idea might work out better than she'd been willing to believe just a few short days ago.

The waitress came. Megan ordered a big bowl of

clam chowder and some crusty homemade bread to go with it.

Thuy ordered just a cup of chowder. "I'm so excited I'm not very hungry," she said.

"I know you're in a hurry to get home," Darren said. "I guess we don't all need to go to Greentree Farm, then come all the way back here. We adults can pick up the boat trailer and camping gear at Fort Ebey, then drive down-island to put the fuel pump in the van. You kids can take the boats and check in with us at the Langley marina just to be sure the van is fixed. Then Sarah and I will drive across on the ferry and meet you at the Madrona Bay marina. How does that sound?"

"Complicated." Peter grinned.

"Fun!" Megan exclaimed. "Thuy, maybe we'll get to meet your grandmother."

"Speaking of Grandmother, I'd better call her again and tell her we're on our way." Dinh excused himself and went to the restaurant's pay phone.

Megan stared out the window at the boats clustered around the floats. "I wonder what will happen to the Sister Susie?"

"The sheriff confiscated her," her stepfather answered. "He'll put her in storage until everything is settled."

"I suppose Dinh and Thuy will have to testify." Thuy's eyes widened in fear, and Megan remembered too late that Thuy's fear of officials was why she'd hidden so long at Fort Ebey. "Of course," she said hastily, "Peter and I were there when Buffalo tried to ram the Good Fortune. We'll be right there beside you to testify too."

"I can't say what might happen," Darren said. "These things sometimes take a long time to move through the system. The sheriff did ask me, Megan, to compliment you on your quick thinking in taking those photos of Buffalo and Ole at the Langley dock. He's keeping copies for evidence." He handed her the package of photographs.

They were still passing the photos around when Dinh returned. "Grandmother asks that you all please stop and let her serve you tea when we get to Madrona Bay."

"We'd love that. But we won't stay long," Sarah said. "You've been gone for more than a week. You have a lot of catching up to do."

~~~~~~~~~~~~~~~~~~~~~~~~~~~~

When they finished eating, the adults left for Fort Ebey. The young people walked to the boats.

"When Megan gets the rest of her pictures developed, we could send you copies," Peter told Thuy. "They'll help you remember this adventure and us."

"I will never forget what's happened this week," said Thuy. "And I'll never, ever, forget you." She gave him a quick hug and sprang aboard the Good Fortune.

Megan caught Peter's eye. She smiled as his ears turned red.

"See you in Langley," Thuy called. Megan tossed the Good Fortune's lines aboard as Dinh started the motor and steered away from the float. Then she helped Peter cast off the lines for their boat. They followed the Good Fortune.

The sky seemed an endless blue; the breeze felt invigorating. Megan wished she could stay on the water forever.

"Want to take over, Megan?"

"I've never steered a boat," she said.

"It's easy. Here, take the wheel." Peter stood beside her as she gingerly turned the wheel a little one way, then the other, and felt the boat respond. She grinned. This was even more fun than driving a car.

"You know," she said to Peter, "I've been thinking about something ... ever since you and Thuy took the rotor out of the distributor. Was I really that hard to get along with?"

"We thought you were," Peter said after a pause. "But you were right too ... I was jealous that you could drive and I couldn't. I'm glad that you have your license. Otherwise we might never have found Dinh."

"Well ... you'll get yours in just a couple of months," Megan said. "And you'll be a good driver too. You're so good with the boat."

"Thanks! You're doing okay yourself."

At the Langley marina they filled the boats' gas tanks then wandered up the hill to the main street. They looked east across the expanse of Puget Sound to the mainland. In the north, the white cone of Mt. Baker anchored the chain of Cascade peaks, a rugged backdrop for green foothills and blue bay waters.

"So many boats," Megan commented. "All going toward the mainland."

"Vacation's over," Peter said in a mournful voice that made them all laugh.

157

After they'd waited more than half an hour, Dinh said, "I hope your parents aren't having trouble."

"No problem," said Peter. "Here comes the van now."

The minivan pulled up beside them, with Megan's mom at the wheel. Darren pulled up right behind with the pickup.

"Hi, kids. Everything okay with the boats?" Darren called. They assured him all was well. "We'll head for the dock then," he said. "There'll be a line-up of holiday traffic at the landing."

The adults waved and pulled away. The young people walked back to the boats, climbed aboard, and motored out across the Sound.

When they reached the big marina at Madrona Bay, Megan helped Peter dock their boat near the launch facility to wait for their parents and the boat trailer. Then they walked toward the dock where the Nguyens were mooring their boat.

They saw a tiny old lady in a long black tunic and cotton trousers hastening down the dock ahead of them. "It's their grandmother," said Peter. Thuy and her brother raced from their boat to hug the little woman.

"They're all talking a mile a minute," Megan commented. "I love happy endings."

Suddenly Thuy broke away and ran to them, her knapsack bouncing on her shoulders. "Look what Grandmother brought me," she cried, waving an envelope. She thrust a sheet of paper at them, laughing and crying at the same time. "Read it."

Together Megan and Peter read the letter.

Dear Miss Nguyen:

Upon the recommendations of your music teacher and our Board of Directors, you are hereby cordially invited to join the Madrona Bay Youth Symphony Orchestra.

The first meeting will be ...

Megan squealed. She grabbed Thuy's hands and whirled her around.

"That's great! Congratulations," Peter said.

"We'll come to all your performances," Megan told her.

Dinh approached and introduced his grandmother, who smiled and spoke in Vietnamese. "She says she is honored to know you. She wishes to thank you for helping us."

"How do you say 'you're welcome' in Vietnamese?" Megan asked.

Dinh told her. She and Peter repeated the syllables as the old lady smiled and nodded some more.

"A neighbor brought Grandmother in his car," Dinh said. "He will take her back to our apartment now. I will go with her if Thuy may ride with you when your parents come."

"Of course she may," Megan answered.

The three friends sat down on the dock to wait.

"I'm so happy. I just have to play my flute," said Thuy. "Do you mind?"

"Please play," Megan said. Peter nodded agreement.

Megan lay back on the warm dock. She folded her hands beneath her head as the notes of Mozart's music soared.

What a summer this had been! Tomorrow would see the start of a new school year with its challenges and excitement. She watched Thuy's delicate fingers coax beautiful music from her flute.

There'd be challenges at home too, of course. But this adventure with Thuy and Peter and Dinh had taught her at least one thing: Jesus could help her conquer any challenge.